WHEN A LOBSTER WHISTLES ON TOP OF A MOUNTAIN THE BALLERINAS WILL DANCE

stories by

ERIN CAMILLE JACKSON

&

AARON A. A. SMITH

FIRST LOBSTERKREATIVE EDITION, SEPTEMBER 2021

This work is fiction.

Library of Congress Control Number:

2021910334

ISBN: 978-1-7372477-0-8

www.instagram.com/aaronaasmith

Contents

CONTENTS

To Aunto

You're still my person

THE WORLD IS A HELLISH PLACE, AND BAD WRITING IS DESTROYING THE QUALITY OF OUR SUFFERING.

—TOM WAITS

The Hungry Ghost

Aaron A. A. Smith

It is said that there are haunted houses

Houses in which people's spirits have passed

Where hungry ghosts dwell

Reliving their deaths over and over in an endless loop

Or wandering back and forth on creaking floors

Searching for something

Ever searching

But it is not you, my dearest one

I lost you in this house

But you are not the hungry ghost

You are beyond all grief and pain

Beyond suffering

Beyond good and evil (I know you would love that line)

It is I

I am the hungry ghost

It is I whose spirit has passed

It is I who relives their death over and over in an endless loop

It is I who wander back and forth on creaking floors searching for something

Ever searching for you

Is this a Prologue or a Short Story?

Aaron A. A. Smith

I don't know. It does serve the function of a prologue, in that it provides an introduction and a bit of context to the following short story anthology. Some of the stories are even specifically mentioned. This little section also touches on some of the key themes and emotions that run through this collection of stories: the bittersweet melancholy of the ephemeral, disconnection, sadness, humor, anxiety, angst, and outright craziness (or eccentricity if this book turns out to be a literary success). Yet these elements are bound together in the form of a narrative, a story unto itself.

So maybe this little introductory overture is a prologue. Maybe it's a short story. Maybe it's some unholy hybrid like a chimera. Maybe it's just antipasti. Or maybe it doesn't matter what you call it. Maybe all that matters is that you enjoy it. That you feel something when you read it, as we felt something when we wrote it. That it's all right here on the pages below. And that all of it is true.

***

The phone wasn't working. I double-tapped the screen and swiped. Nothing. I tapped and swiped again. And again. Still nothing. The damn thing had been fine when I set it on the bookshelf the night before, but now it was a goner. Kaput. Dead, dead, deadsky as Beetlejuice would say.

In the normal course of events, a dead phone is an inconvenience at the very least. But in my current predicament, it was a disaster. I had spent the better part of a year using it to write my contribution to this short story collection. Most of "La Chatte Grise," about half of "Room 7," and the beginning of "Sadaharu's Dream" were locked in the limbo of a dead phone.

I should have known better. I should have copied my writing in a notebook each night. Should have. In theory I should have backed them up on a computer or a memory card. In theory, that is. As a practical matter, I would have had better luck backing up an eighteen-wheeler into a compact parking spot. I'm a brick and mortar kind of man. A luddite. A technophobe. Feel free to pick a metaphor for a man out of time. A man whose time has passed. All the more reason to keep my work out of the hands of the machines. Not that they literally have hands. Well, some of them do. Those vaguely disturbing clasping metal ones that look like a prop from *The Terminator*. But that's not the point.

For the sake of context, I should probably mention that the machines and I are mortal enemies. They have been firing petty volleys of aggression and annoyance at me for years. Like the way my old car had some weird electrical short that required me to hammer the console like Fonzie from *Happy Days* in order to turn on the radio. Or the way the current car won't eject that one CD, and idles in an unnerving way no matter how many times it goes in to the repair shop. Or the way the microwave up and stopped working after only a year of use, followed almost immediately by the sudden demise of the oven. Or the way my old DVD player used to display the word "loading" on the TV screen while stubbornly refusing to play the disc. After a while, the word ceased to have any meaning in the English language. It began to ring out in my mind as the name of some obscure Chinese city. *Loading… Loa-ding.* Then there was the time the dryer broke, then caught on fire when the repair kid tried to fix it. *Und so weiter,* as the Germans say.

But perhaps the most grating of the machines' offenses are the petty banalities that they fling. Like how the automatic soap and water dispensers refuse to acknowledge my presence. They work fine for the next guy, but not for me. It's as if they are silently affirming the existential truth of my own non-existence.

So, in retrospect, it was probably unwise to place a year's worth of work in the hands of a computer phone. A technological device. A machine. A hostile entity. Yet there I was, trying to coax that phone back to life long enough to retrieve my writing. At least "The Ballerina and the Music Box," "The Lanai," and "The Prisoner and the Lion" were tucked safely away in my notebook. I had put a lot of work into those stories. But I had also put a lot of work into the stories on my phone. The thought of doing it all again…

I tapped the phone again. Again, it stubbornly refused to respond. I wildly poked the on/off switch and the volume control in random directions, patterns, and orbits. For a brief moment, the screen flickered with a spark of life, then it turned blue and died once more.

Maybe the battery was the problem. I stared at the phone. There was no way I was going to go prodding around inside that contraption, so we (when I say 'we,' I do not mean the 'royal we,' rather I am referring to myself and my co-author) drove the disturbingly idling car down to the nearest AT&T store. The kid who worked there popped open the back of the phone, removed the battery, and put it back inside. The phone came to life. *Result! Victory!* Or so it seemed. About two minutes after I left the store, the phone's screen turned blue. It was dead again.

Now I was in a spy novel situation. Critical information had been embedded and lost in an advanced technological device. I, the protagonist of the story, had to repair the device, or at least extract the vital data. On this, all depended. How else was I to save the free world and rescue the post-Soviet ballerinas? How, I ask you?!

And what was the mood of this spy novel to be? The tone? John Le Carre'? Ian Fleming? Maybe something more blunt, like Darth Vader bellowing "I want those plans!" And where the hell was R2-D2 when you needed him?

So on the next day, I downed a whiskey and a vodka soda, and girded my loins for an excursion to the Best Buy in Mission Valley. *"Best Buy. Mission Valley. Shit,"* growled Martin Sheen.

Mission Valley is San Diego's aging old whore of a shopping district. In decades past, she was considered a vibrant and glamorous hub, nestled between Jack Murphy Stadium and Hotel Circle. But over the years, her luster faded. The Padres moved to a beautiful new ballpark downtown. The Chargers moved to L.A. The hotels are mostly empty. Now Mission Valley is a depressing cluster of malls, strewn about like crop plats around an unnecessarily and incomprehensibly tortuous pretzel-knot of streets. There is a vague sense of death in the air. Something akin to walking into a town that time left behind. But it still has the malls, the chain restaurants, the movie theatres, the soulless office buildings and soulless 'luxury' apartments. Which is to say that it is still crowded, and therefore a pain in the ass to navigate. Especially during rush hour, or, say, the week before Christmas. Which of course it was.

It didn't feel like Christmas this year. Sure, Christmas decorations had been gradually infiltrating the stores since before Halloween. Hokey carols had violated the airwaves of the rock stations on the radio. But it still didn't feel like Christmas. I had seen images of Tokyo, Moscow, Paris, and London on TV and the internet. These images, these places felt like Christmas to me. But here where I was, I couldn't feel it. It was the same vacant drudgery. Sure, there were isolated pockets around town that felt like Christmas: the lights at the San Diego Zoo and Balboa Park. The poinsettia tree in Little Italy. The view from the rooftop of my building encompassing the red and green lights beaming from the skyscraper across the street, the big red tree of lights beside the harbor, and the faint white illumination of the lights atop the Hotel del Coronado, barely visible on the horizon. But these little spots seemed like nothing more than anomalies in the fabric of time and space. They did not reflect reality.

In reality, we were at a Best Buy in a mall the week before Christmas, trying to extract critical data from a treacherous, technologically-advanced espionage machine. But the overlords at Best Buy informed me that that they were not in the espionage business and did not work on deadly technological devices of this particular brand. Must be some sort of exclusive licensing contract with specific treacherous, technologically-advanced espionage machine companies.

Next, off to an AT&T store at an adjacent strip mall. There they informed me that they too were not in the espionage business. Rather, they were exclusively in the retail business. They did, however, direct me to a repair shop in the main mall in Mission Valley. The mall with the big movie theatre. And the Target. And the Outback Steak House, of course.

At the repair shop, I unsheathed my phone and presented it to the guy behind the counter. He froze, agawp and agog in amazement at the rare and ancient artifact in my possession. A brilliant beam of blinding white light flooded down from the heavens and shone upon the holy techno device. It was like I was Sir Percival returning triumphantly from my quest to capture the Holy Grail. And this old, outdated phone was the legendary icon itself. *I know I just switched literary genres. First I was speaking in spy novel analogies. Now it's Arthurian legends. And I'm going to do it again.*

The guy behind the counter marveled at the archaic, old dude phone. "I haven't seen one of these in forever," he said. He called to his colleague: "Hey, have you ever seen one of these?"

"No," she answered.

"Look what good shape it's in. Even the charger plug looks good."

Now they were both gazing reverently at my arcane archaeological artifact of a phone. I halfway expected Indiana Jones to burst into the scene shouting things like "It belongs in a museum!" or "Don't look at it Marion! Keep your eyes shut!"

But that didn't happen. What did happen was the repair guy poked around at the phone, and the blue screen ominously appeared again. "That's not good," he said. "That's what we call the blue screen of death." Apparently that is a thing. Who knew? The long and short of it is that when the blue screen appears on a computer phone, you're screwed. There is pretty much nothing to be done. That device has flatlined, with its arcane secrets trapped inside. Maybe a temporary solder job could get her going long enough to extract the data. Maybe. But a job of that magnitude was beyond the expertise of anyone in this particular store. This particular mall. This particular ageing whore of a shopping district. And the cost of such a job could very well turn out to be prohibitive anyway.

Thwarted again. I was starting to feel like a hardboiled detective chasing down a breadcrumb trail of clues that kept leading from one dead end to another. *I told you I was going to switch genres again.*

One last shot.

Over lunch that week, my co-author's father had mentioned that there was a cell phone repair specialty shop in Little Italy. I figured I might as well give it a try. One last desperate, Doug Flutie-esque Hail Mary pass before the clock ran out. So the next evening, I headed to Little Italy.

In its former glory, Little Italy had consisted of a collection of old school Italian restaurants frequented by old Italian guys, other old guys, day drunks, assorted characters and caricatures, various mutant life forms, and a rotating stream of tourists who all somehow seemed vaguely Canadian.

Then came the Great Hipster Invasion. I'm pretty sure it started with the Saturday farmer's market. Then came the Ballast Point local craft brewery (Hipsters conspicuously and pretentiously gather around local craft breweries. It's a common trait of their species). None stood against them. Once the first dominos fell, the whole neighborhood was lost. Son of a bitch. Eisenhower was right.

Now the neighborhood is lined with fungible eateries that are either painted a garish, blinding white like a dentist's office in Heaven, or are decked in dark wood tones amidst a labyrinth of gaudy, superfluous, nonfunctional exposed brass. And all packed to the rafters with skinny jeans and meticulously over-groomed beards. And those ubiquitous haircuts that are clipped just a bit too short in the back and on the sides, but are long and slathered on top and always remind me of Hitler. Wait a minute! Hitler… Hister… Hipster…We may have misinterpreted Nostradamus.

But this particular night was a cold, drizzly December weeknight. Not too crowded. The parking was ok.

I walked down India Street beneath a string of Christmas lights that ran all the way up and down the main drag. Past the poinsettia tree. Through the tiny anomaly in time and space that let Christmas in for a moment. Then into the phone repair shop. It was small and neat inside. Simple, straightforward, and unpretentious.

I explained my top secret mission to the man at the counter. He said they had a repairman who just might be able to get the phone up and working, at least long enough to retrieve the data. We'd know sometime the next day. So I handed over the phone, signed the repair invoice, and headed home.

***

I always have the vague sense that I'm standing in the on-deck circle, waiting for my turn at bat. But my turn never comes. I'm left standing there in an eternal limbo of nerves. Now that sense was palpable. It had grown as acutely sharp as the edge of a tanto. I needed to distract myself. To blow off some steam.

I took the elevator down to the gym in my apartment building, got in a heavy leg and shoulder workout, and popped back up to my flat. I stripped off my sweat-drenched white tank top and downed a couple of vodka sodas. And brooded. I felt trapped and stifled and anxious. I needed some air. It was cold and drizzly that night. I would likely have the rooftop to myself. I could breathe in the crisp, rainy air and look at the city skyline from twenty floors up without disturbance.

I left my flat and walked down the hall to the elevator. I pressed the roof button and waited. *Ding!* The doors slid open. I stepped inside.

Ventus! Dominus! I knew that soundtrack. It was the soundtrack of the dreaded *Spoildus Bratticus Suburbanus Americanus,* the common American undisciplined suburban hellspawn in its natural environment. The unholy offspring of lame, post-Dr. Spock parents and a jackal. Damian turned legion. Such undisciplined hellspawn are always honed and accompanied by at least one undisciplinarian suburbanite parent. In this case, it was a typical suburban soccer mom type. The type that wears yoga pants to PTA meetings. The type that has neighbor friends and couple friends who all gather around a box of wine set on top of a travertine counter. The type that thinks a Lexus and a Berber carpet represent the height of luxury. The type who has their walls painted beige, but calls it something 'fancier' like Swiss mocha. The type who never corrects or disciplines their children, never says "no" or "stop it" out of fear of damaging their extraordinary child's fragile self-esteem. That's how you make a—

Ventus! Dominus!

The elevator doors slid shut. I was trapped for a good dozen floors. *"Elevator. Shit,"* Martin Sheen growled again.

The child-star of *The Omen* began to loudly and repeatedly blare a shrill, mind-numbing chant. It rang through my ears and brain, but the actual words were unintelligible.

The closest to any actual words that my throbbing ears could decipher were "Where's the woad?" *Woad?*

Woad is a blue hallucinogenic paint that the ancient Celto-Pictish tribespeople smeared on their bodies before battle. They believed it bestowed them with strength, courage, and mystical powers. In reality, they were just tripping balls. And if they sounded anything like this human child version of a shrill, blaring, repetitive European ambulance siren, it's no wonder Hadrian built that damn wall.

Somehow the creature's soccer mom/keeper was able to decipher its mad and cryptic ramblings. It seemed that Damian had gotten it into his 666-marked head that my knee-length basketball shorts were in fact underwear. And not only was his soccer mom/keeper making no effort to disabuse him of the notion, she actually seemed to be placidly endorsing it. "You know how people walk around in their underwear in their own houses?" she chirped cheerily (and apparently completely unperturbed at the idea of a grown man riding up and down the elevator of the building where she and her child reside in his underwear). "He's in his house."

What!? The freaking things are clearly outerwear! They go down to my knees! People parade back and forth from the rooftop hot tub in skimpy swimwear all the time, but somehow basketball shorts are underwear!?

"That's underwear," suburban demonseed Damian announced with all the certainty of a judge decreeing law, finally eschewing his native infernal tongue in favor of the English language. He wasn't alarmed or upset or anything. He just wanted to proclaim that my workout shorts were underwear in his loudest and clearest voice. He did so with all the enthusiasm, surety, confidence, and wrongness of a neophyte congregant preaching 'the word.' And again, his suburban soccer mom/keeper said nothing. So I guess there's some blaring megaphone of a kid in my building who thinks there's a big, long-haired man with tattoos who roams the elevators in his underwear. But everybody's cool with it. Awesome.

Finally and mercifully the elevator bell dinged. Suburban soccer mom/Damian keeper and I exchanged perfunctory goodnights, and the unholy microcosm of suburban life exited the elevator and this story.

The doors closed and the elevator continued upward toward the roof. The doors opened and I stepped out into the cool, drizzly air. The night was calm and quiet high above the bustle of the city streets. A soft, somehow comforting, rain fell. The roof was vacant. Not a soul to bother me. Silence at last.

I walked across the wet patio tiles and stood by the rail of the roof. I looked at the cityscape and beyond. The red and green lights beaming on the surface of the building across the street. The shining red lights of the giant Christmas tree next to the convention center. The green lights of Emerald Plaza. The dark waters of the harbor and the arc of the Coronado Bridge. And on the far horizon, the faint white glow of lights on the roof of the Hotel del Coronado. A funny little picture of Christmas in the aggregate. A fractal of the anomalous rift in time and space.

I stood gazing out over the skyline for a long time. Head whirling. That feeling rose again. I was standing in the on deck circle. But my turn to bat would never come. *All that work. Gone.*

I stood in the rain a moment longer. *Moonlight and Rain.* But I couldn't find the moon. It was hidden behind dark gray clouds.

Then I headed back down to my apartment to do the only thing I could.

***

TRANSITION TO PANDA.

Standing there alone on the page of my notebook, the words looked like stage directions from *The Winter's Tale* if it had been written in Japan. Which, of course, it wasn't. The jotting in question was in fact a note to remind myself where to pick up in writing "Room 7." I had written the rest of the story on my phone. So, at this point it may as well have been words spoken into the wind before a drunken nap.

The panda in question is a character in “Room 7.” To be more precise, she is a stuffed panda modeled after a plushy that resides in my apartment. Naturally, I chose to insert her in a gritty yet bittersweet contemporary *noir* story.

I had a lot of work to do, but at least I had a jumping-off point. I introduced the panda again, though a bit differently this time. I gave her some added backstory. I think she would be pleased.

I finished the next scene. It was late. I had been burning the midnight oil again. And my version of the midnight oil burns way past midnight. It’s something like the literary equivalent of the Maccabees’ oil. You might expect it to burn out around midnight, but it actually keeps flickering until about four or five in the morning.

My head was going fuzzy. I needed sleep. No matter what, the next day was going to be long and I was going to be slinging a lot of ink.

***

The conclusion to the infamous Ordeal of the Phone (as Tolkien may have called it) proved to be triumphant, albeit anti-climactic. The repair shop called me on my co-author's phone. The repairman had managed to temporarily Macguyver the phone back to life by soldering some chip to another doohickey to the bad mutha board on the mother ship. At least that's the technical description of the process as I understand it.

The problem was that the fix was temporary. When the one doohickey inevitably lost its connection to the other doohickey, the phone would die again, likely forever this time. And like Arnie from *What's Eating Gilbert Grape,* it could go at any time.

The rest of the night surged by in a blur. I retrieved the phone, headed home, drank a pot of coffee, poured a vodka soda, grabbed a pen and notebook, and delicately placed the phone on the arm of the couch. I tentatively activated the device like a bomb squad officer trying not to trigger an explosive device.

The screen lit up. Everything was there. All my work. Now it was a race to hand-write it all down before the phone died.

I wrote almost nonstop deep into the night. My eyes went bleary. A writing blister chafed my finger. No time to rest. *You're on the final lap. Put your head down and push on.*

And at last, sometime before four in the morning, the race was over. I had won. Everything I had written on my phone was now in my notebook. Safe and sound. If the cat didn't eat it. She has a penchant for gnawing on notebooks.

So, in the end, the book you are about to read turned out exactly as planned. No need to recreate stories. No unintended additions, subtractions, or alterations. Well, I suppose there are two unintended additions to this collection that were inspired by the Ordeal of the Phone. One is a bit of extra backstory for a stuffed panda (and who doesn't want more panda backstory?). The other is the very introduction/prologue/short story/unholy chimera/antipasti you are reading right now.

***

And now the introductory narrative section of our program draws to a close. Time to clear the antipasti plates. The main course is about to be served (it may include lobster). The opening band has finished their set. Flick your bics as the headliners take the stage. Or whichever metaphor feels apt. But I think I'm partial to this one…

Ladies and gentlemen, please take your seats and silence your cell phones (we all know what a bother they can be). Lobsters, ballerinas, stuffed pandas, talking cats, and other players to your places. The big red Bolshoi Ballet/David Lynch curtain is about to rise. Dear reader, I hope you enjoy the show. We'll meet for drinks during the *intermezzo*.

Aaron A. A. Smith, 2019

LOBSTERS

Erin Camille Jackson

Restaurant's lobster tank was dark and cold. It sat in a lovely corner, flanked by palm plants. It gurgled, musically, under the drone of piano notes, tired conversation, and clinking silverware. The lobsters in the tank often drowsed in crustacean complacency or drifted, without intention, past the glass that housed them. That is the pleasant impression that they projected to the finely dressed patrons who, on occasion, peered into their aquatic realm.

Churchill was the leader of the lobsters. He had lived in that tank longer than he could remember. He'd lived someplace before Restaurant, but that fact didn't occupy his mind. He was a practical lobster, and the well-being of his troops was his highest concern.

"Dignity and discipline," was one of his mottos, and he was frequently heard to grumble such as he drifted back and forth across the tank's chilly waters.

At that time, Churchill was responsible for four other lobsters. They were not his first spiny battalion, but something about this group was special. They may not have been the fastest swimmers or the quickest wits, but they had formed the kind of bond that constituted lobster loyalty at its finest. It was a most noble emotion.

Churchill's troops consisted of Harlstons, his second in command; Rocky, a tough creature caught off the Jersey Shore; Hollywood, a lobster overly fond of the sparkling pebbles that lined the tank's floor; and Gator. Gator barely counted as a troop since he seemed to be incapable of voluntary movement. He was the most rotund lobster Churchill had ever encountered. Such was Churchill's band of lobsters.

Restaurant was frequently crowded. The tuxedo clad flitted around between tables, deftly avoiding collisions, while acrobatically balancing massive silver ovals on both arms. They seemed to know exactly the maneuvers the others were about to execute. Restaurant's noise rose, some nights, to a thunderous uproar. No individual sounds distinguished themselves from the horde. And yet, to Churchill's amazement, the business of serving and clearing tables proceeded without incident.

On such harrowing evenings, after Churchill had ordered his troops to bed, he would press his hardened face against the smooth glass and observe the pageantry of it all. Through the water's distortion he perceived something distinguished. He recognized what he came to believe was a military precision. There was order and unity of purpose to the proceedings. It caused him to raise his pointy chin just a touch higher with pride in restaurant's efficiency.

***

One afternoon, as Churchill was putting the others through their daily paces, he noticed a distinct shift in Restaurant's usual goings on. Most afternoons the tuxedos would rhythmically begin setting out the linens and silver for the dinner service. They were so familiar with these tasks that no great effort need be expended. Business as usual. All calm on the Restaurant front. But, on this otherwise unremarkable afternoon, there was a clambering about at lunatic pace. Linens were removed and repositioned. Two of the tuxedos actually broke formation and, hence, crashed into one another. This sent a bombardment of napkins parachuting to the floor, carpeting a tragic mass of china cup casualties. Churchill was stunned and a bit embarrassed to have borne witness to such floundering.

Apparently, the disaster had launched such a shock wave of horror that it aroused the attentions of the one who lived in the kitchen, behind the swinging doors. This was the white coated man with the oddly tall hat, the one the tuxedos called Chef. He was rarely observed by the lobsters, but rumors abounded that he was truly evil. The only times he ever emerged from his kitchen home he did so with war cries and flaming eyes…carrying a huge glittering blade in one hand and a rag in the other. Presumably the rag was to wipe the blood from his pristine coat should he find it necessary to dismember anyone with his knife. He emerged in just such a manner that afternoon. Churchill halted his troops mid-march to observe the potential gore before them.

A deep guttural growl rumbled up from the belly of Chef. It grew in volume and intensity until it became coupled with a hawk-like screech. Then the two sounds converged into such a demonic scream that the crystal chandeliers rattled like icicles above the tables and tank. Gator's claws quivered as he fruitlessly attempted to dig a hole through the pebbles in which to hide. The two tuxedos who had caused this onslaught of wrath leapt to their feet. Bowing their heads, they ran backward out the door, gasping pitiful apologies for their very birth. Presumably, they were in search of a broom, or a broom closet in which to hide. Chef uttered a few curses under his breath before tromping heavily back into his kitchen. Churchill located Gator, his head tucked beneath his claws. Rocky tried to force his comrade to attention, but to no avail.

Churchill pondered all these events quietly for a moment, trying to concentrate over the din of Gator's weeping protests and Rocky's impatient demands. He needed to figure out what was happening out there. There was a tingling in his tail that had, in times past, served to alert him to certain danger. It was a soldier's instinct. Churchill grumbled softly to himself before turning to his number two, Harlstons. He needed a good chap on this assignment, and Harlston's was by far the best.

"Err...her...humph...herm," Churchill cleared his throat in preparation for addressing his troops.

"Yes, well, it has come to my attention that we may have a situation out there. We need to gather more intelligence before constructing our plan of action, if in fact action needs taking."

The battalion of lobsters immediately fell into formation. Each lobster directed his eyes quite as straight forward as was possible for a crustacean, while forcing their antennae up, stiffly, in salute. They eagerly awaited Churchill's orders. Even Hollywood resisted the desperate urge to confiscate a remarkably shiny pebble that rested temptingly at his left claw. The call of the treasure was great, but not so great as his respect for the mighty Churchill. He was a solider after all.

Once Churchill was sure that he had their complete attention he began his routine of pacing from one end of the line to the other and back again. The movement always organized and ordered his thoughts. He would pace without speaking for as long as it took to become one with the rhythm of what he was about say. This process also allowed Gator a little extra time to wrap his brain around what was going on. If he spoke too soon Gator would still be daydreaming of chow time and bubbles. Churchill let out an almost inaudible sigh and turned to address his lobsters.

"Today we have witnessed chaos in what is usually a well-oiled machine. The tuxedos are not calm. They are afraid of something…something that is coming during this evening's dinner service battle." He paused to let this sink in.

"Now, we have observed many a dinner service battle. And these battles have almost entirely been victories. We are proud of Restaurant and of the brave tuxedos in her service. In the face of this current incident we have no other choice than to arm ourselves with as much information as possible. We want no surprises!"

Churchill stood in front of Harlstons, looked him hard in the eye, and delivered his orders. "Officer Harlstons, it is your duty to discover the nature of the current situation and report back to me, ASAP. Do you understand?"

Harlstons raised himself even straighter and clicked his claws together before launching up into the water and swimming off in the direction of the rear tank wall. The others remained at attention while Churchill resumed his pacing and grumbling. Harlstons swam with all his lobster might, satisfied with the huge honor he had been granted. He would not let them down.

It was not a far swim, so Harlstons was shortly situated up against the rear glass of the tank. This glass faced the front door, where on a little podium there was always a large printed sign. The lobsters had discovered, over time, that this sign was changed every day. Apparently, the sign's purpose was to inform the customers and the tuxedos as to the particulars of the dinner service battle for the evening. It listed any unusual titles for the battle and often any special items to be served.

Churchill and his troops had concluded that battles with particular titles were much larger than those simply named for the date. For example, Harlstons recalled that the great Christmas battle of just under two months ago had been enormous. Restaurant had been bombarded by customers and had even had to call up extra tuxedos to fill in the ranks. Conversely, the minor battle of Wednesday, last week, was so small it barely roused the attentions of the lobsters at all. Harlstons felt certain that tonight's battle must be one of the massive titled engagements, perhaps even bigger than the Christmas battle!

Now, vertically, he swam to the surface of the cool water. His antennae poked into the air, waggling frantically, as he propped one, then another spiny claw on the tank's rim. This was the easy part. In order to properly read the words of the sign Harlstons had to hoist his head up into the air and dangle there, supported by his claws. He'd done this many times before, but each time a terror of failure gripped his salty heart. It would be a source of immense distress to dishonor himself in the eyes of Churchill. In fact, Harlstons feared nothing in his watery world more than to fail his leader and commander. How many dinner battles had they endured side by side?

"Well," thought Harlstons, "This shall be but another."

He located the sign. Instead of being white, with the usual elegant black printing, it was a most garish shade of pink. The lettering was deep red and glittered under the chandelier's light. It was garish! Harlstons recoiled. Where was the dignity? Hollywood would have loved it, just like he loved all his silly colorful pebbles. Hollywood was so fond of the shiny things that he had even slung a piece of seaweed across his belly in which he stored his collection. Harlstons had frequently seen him staring longingly at the sparkle of silverware adorning Restaurant's tables. The whole thing seemed rather silly to Harlstons, but it was none of his business. His business was to read this damnable sign and report back, post haste.

"Ah ha! It does have a title!" He cried, pleased with his correct assumption.

"This shall be henceforth known as…The Battle of Valentine's Day!" Harlstons paused in his reading just a moment, for dramatic effect, before perusing the list of items to be served. Most of the items were either beyond Harlston's experience or interest. There was a creamed this, a sautéed that, and a few things that he simply ignored. Just as he was about to sink back into the water and return to the front he noticed something in print much larger than the other items. It was familiar. Harlstons halted everything. He read it again…

LOBSTER

Harlstons plopped down into the waters. He quickly gathered his wits and garnered his soldier's skills. His training had prepared him to thrive in a crisis. He had to hasten back to the front to warn the other troops. Churchill would know precisely what must be done. Harlstons did not doubt for a second that their great leader would act swiftly and without fear. Harlstons swam faster than any lobster had ever swum. His tail ached, but performed admirably. He could almost see the line waiting anxiously for his scouting report. They were just around the big mossy boulder. He rounded the corner…

The waters were rocked by the plunge of one huge ugly hand, then another. The beastly hands spread their tentacle-like fingers and groped through the cool wetness of the lobster tank. They crashed into the seaweed and scraped along the pebbles. The hands were so close to the line of troops! It was happening already. Harlstons felt the heat of shame. He had failed Churchill.

"Swim! Swim, troops!" Harlstons yelled as he charged toward his comrades.

Churchill had already gathered the lobsters into battle formation. He was barking orders as he dodged the grasping giant's paws. Hollywood cried out in terror. He seemed to have forgotten his formations and was swimming in frantic zigzags and spirals. Gator was the first to fall victim. He was so large and slow that it made him an easy target. One hand snatched him out of the water and thrust him through the air into the bowels of a shallow container. Harlstons found Rocky, and the two of them steam rolled toward the resubmurged hands.

Churchill raged, "Charge! By God, charge the bastards!" But it did no good.

Harlstons tried in vain to pinch the hands, only to realize that his great claws were bound by horrible rubber bands! He was helpless! Out of the water, into the bucket, flew brave Harlstons and fiery Rocky. Rocky uttered a cry of wrath and let loose such curses as have never been heard by man nor beast!

Only Hollywood and the great Churchill remained to fight. As Churchill stared, horrified, at his last remaining troop being hoisted from the water he knew what he must do. He charged the offending hands with all his lobster might. He uttered the primal cry of menace that signaled violent attack. Inflamed by noble indignation, he collided with the fleshy fingers of the empty hand. His claws being bound, he battered the hand with his crustacean tail. The usually placid waters churned and splashed like a hurricane at sea, but Churchill continued his attack.

All at once the thrashing ceased. Churchill had been grabbed and was being wretchedly lifted into the air. The insult was spectacular. The great shame of it all. But brave Churchill knew that if his troops had any chance of survival in this battle of all battles they would need his unflinching leadership. He must rejoin his fellow combatants. So, into the air he rose and dutifully allowed himself to be transported into the kitchen. This battle had not yet begun.

***

Behind the swinging doors, the kitchen was a steaming, sputtering, bustling overload of fragrances and sounds. That's not to mention the dizzying race of white clad kitchen staff. Chef was at the head of it all, constantly checking each station for potential disasters. Under Chef there were two sous chefs, with various missions, and one particularly soggy looking man in charge of all the dishes. This last one lorded over the sink, which was a vast steel pit crowned with a coiled snake of a faucet. Above the sink shone the lone window. It was always kept cracked just enough to allow a mocking breeze to rustle through the air, whispering of other worlds not consumed by heat and culinary odors.

***

Churchill quickly observed the terrain. His military mind evaluated the situation with a clipped efficiency seldom known in other crustaceans. He knew his troops were dutifully awaiting his orders. He must rise to the task.

The lobster troops had organized themselves into ranks, albeit shaking and terrified ranks. Harlstons alone did not quake. He stood at attention, prepared to execute his leader's orders. He had no doubt they would triumph in this greatest of battles.

"I will tell of this day to the coming generations. I will speak of the honor of my fellow lobsters. I will share my pride at having served under such a leader as Churchill."

Churchill cleared his throat and addressed his audience with authority and deepest respect.

"Lobsters, today is the day that all our training will be rewarded. All our earlier battles have been but preparation for this moment. We are lobsters. We are not clams, with our foolish shells dug into the sand. Stupid animals. We are not shrimp…the name itself says it all. We are not crabs; a frivolous group of creatures, too disorganized and weak to achieve the victory. We are lobsters. And this is our time.

History will speak in reverent tones of this greatest day, this epic battle…This Lobster Uprising!"

On this final point he raised his banded claws in the air as the troops roared with a battle cry so visceral that the water itself echoed its holler. Rocky snarled as only a lobster can snarl. His muscles were twitching for action. Harlston's heart beat like a kettle drum to the rhythm of a lobster's sacred march. They anxiously awaited their orders.

Churchill began, "Lobsters, I will be brief, but exact in conveying our plan of action. Time is of the essence!" He cleared his throat and raised his massive fore claw importantly.

"See that open window over the sink? That is our target. Stay on target, my troops. Stay on target."

The brave lobsters turned to observe the aforementioned window. Target sighted.

"Now, outside that window is a stream that leads back to the ocean. We must traverse the treacherous countertop without recapture, climb out that window, and swim to the freedom we so rightly deserve." Churchill waited as his troops nodded. They were excellent soldiers.

"To begin, you must clip these bands that restrain our mighty claws. As we do this I shall instruct you in the rest of the plan. Act quickly my fellows. The enemy is at hand."

Churchill's plan was bold. The kitchen staff was all around them. Luckily these fools underestimated the fortitude of a crustacean crusade. If they could avoid notice their plan might succeed. Chef was the biggest threat. His malice was legendary.

Each lobster clipped another's bands and one by one climbed over each other's backs, out of the wretched container. A ladle lay beside the horrible boiling pot. In order for the last lobster, Churchill, to escape the others dragged the ladle over and dropped it into the container. It was not a perfect ladder, but it was all they had. The heavy metal ladle took great effort to lift and hoist, being a good deal longer than any one lobster himself. In an unfortunate moment of gravity the cumbersome ladle slipped just enough to clank hideously against the edge of the container. Oh, the cacophony of clang! The sound would tremor forever in their brains. The kitchen around them was rendered silent audience to the telltale ringing of their plan. As one evil legion, the kitchen staff turned upon the escaping crustaceans. So the battle had truly begun…

Immediately, the two sous chefs were upon them. Their eyes were wild from starvation and degradation. They were quick. Chef had trained them well. Instinctively each grabbed a razor-sharp knife and brandished it at the noble lobsters. They wanted blood!

"Onward troops! This is our moment. Keep moving forward!" Churchill bellowed from the miserable container.

Harlstons' confidence was reinvigorated by the sound of his commander's voice. Black eyes narrowed. He could sense the other lobsters' fight instinct take hold. They were a well-groomed battalion facing a charging enemy.

"Now!" Harlstons and Churchill commanded in unison.

Oh, the poetry of motion. Not one movement wasted.

A serrated knife zoomed past Hollywood's head, missing him by a whisper. Hollywood didn't falter, even as his precious pebble pouch tumbled to the floor, spilling its beloved shinys onto the field of battle. They would be much mourned casualties of this war.

"Bastard People!"

His beautifully manicured claw clasped a particularly pudgy potato chunk off the cutting board. He flung the bulbous vegetable, full force, at the churlish Chef's vile head. Between the bloodshot eyes! It hit its mark. Chef stumbled two steps back, nearly tumbling out of his Danish clogs.

"Ha ha! You are a villain!" Hollywood sang out with animalistic pride.

"Yes, my good fellow! Have at the scum!" Cheered Churchill as he maneuvered the ladle in the container.

A second culinary enemy charged at the fearless troops. His knife was at the ready to avenge his injured colleague. But the lobsters were faster. Rocky launched a barrage of fresh onion skins into his face, blinding him long enough for Harlstons to torpedo a rather impressive carrot sharply into his throat. The foolish bastard doubled over, hideously pawing at this neck, gasping for air.

Gator bombarded the now recovering first sous chef with celery and radish grenades, slowing his approach. Gator moved with such a fury as never could have been anticipated. His training had taken over. He was more machine than lobster!

"That's it! I knew you had it in you!" Churchill was now painfully climbing the ladle, which he had propped up against the container's edge nearest the pot of boiling water.

More vegetables flew through the heated air. A brutal salad attack kept the chefs at bay. They reloaded their wicked hands with the malevolent knives of their trade, but still the lobsters held them off.

Out of the corner of Churchill's always observant eye he saw the soggy dish washer staring dumbly at the scene.

He had not moved to aid his fellow kitchen mates. Churchill observed a change in the overworked man. This man was ready to flee. Maybe they should have paid him better, Churchill conjectured. The man was ready to abandon his post. It was the opportunity Churchill knew the troops needed for escape!

"Forward lobsters! Keep moving!" He shouted from atop the ladle.

At the same time, the dishwasher up and fled the scene of battle, screaming like the coward he was. This left the troops a clear shot at the window. It was their best chance. The two sous chefs were hastily selecting their knives. The vegetable ammunition was nearly depleted.

"Troops, Go, Go, Go! Forward now! It is your moment!" Churchill ordered.

The lobsters were instantly on the move. Harlstons pushed his comrades past him in order to bring up the rear. He saw the evil head Chef hastening toward their position. Chef was far swifter than either of the sous chefs! His eyes blazed with the flame of a man possessed by demonic insanity.

"Hurry Troops!" Harlstons cried.

Churchill saw the cleaver gleam in Chef's highly skilled hand. He was almost upon the lobsters! Churchill looked from his troops to the lunatic beast approaching them. They would never make it in time. Chef was joined by his mangled sous chefs, and they were surging toward the lobsters' position. His troops must not fail! This battle could not be lost in this final strike. Those bravest of comrades! His bravest of comrades!

Churchill knew what he must do. It only took a moment to decide. He was their leader. Their noble commander. Churchill jumped to the rim of the boiling pot of water. The steam singed his back. It was horrifically hot. Hell is hot.

The culinarians charged at his lobsters. This was it. It was the moment.

"Onward to freedom! Never surrender! You are lobsters. Do not forget. You are lobsters!" And with that final battle cry Churchill leapt majestically into the air, the steam billowing below his tail. He raised his glorious claws, spread eagled, and dove tremendously into the molten pot below.

The force of his mighty dive splashed a lava flow of boiling water skyward. Its burning fury found its target, drenching Chef in scalding liquid. He fell to the floor, screaming and clutching his face. His minions halted their attack and looked in horror at their wounded master. Knives clattered to the floor. All this took but an instant. In that instant of chaos the lobster troops reached the open window, breathless. Saved by the distraction, they thrust themselves, one by one, into the precious open water.

Harlstons, last of the lobsters to climb to freedom, turned to glance at the place where his mighty leader had sacrificed himself that they might survive. He felt a dark, stabbing heartbreak at the incredible loss of his commander, his friend.

"This will never be forgotten. You will always live, for us. This day, this battle, will serve to create future generations of lobsters who have bravery and nobility. You will be remembered. I will remember you."

Harlstons leapt out the window into the cool water. It splashed up in the air and sparkled with light.

The Ballerina and the Music Box

Aaron A. A. Smith

Inside the clear glass globe that was the only home she had ever known, a perfect tiny ballerina danced to the melancholy chimes of an exquisitely crafted music box. The tiny ballerina knew nothing of the outside world, nor did she need to. All that she loved and needed lay within the confines of her glass globe.

She lived in a cozy little room, filled with all the amenities her heart could desire. She had a soft bed, covered with fluffy stuffed animals that she cuddled for comfort; a bookshelf full of books; a bedside table and lamp; a red upholstered reclining chair; a costuming space. And all rested atop a little music box, like a world sitting astride the shell of a turtle.

Of particular reverence to the tiny ballerina was the corner of her room that she reserved for the design and creation of her costumes. There she kept a pencil and sketch pad; a sewing machine; beads, sequins, and crystals of various size and shape; and several swatches of fabric. The tiny ballerina loved to sift through the precious fabric, selecting a favorite color or pattern, feeling the texture of the cloth with her fingertips, imagining music and dance, letting inspiration and emotion wash over her. Then she would determinedly sketch her costume designs, measure and cut the fabric, and painstakingly sew the cloth into her latest costume.

As time passed, the tiny ballerina created many lovely costumes in an array of designs and colors. Some ruffled with the familiar frills of a traditional tutu. Some were flowing and diaphanous. Some gradually transitioned from one color to another in a gentle gradient like a brilliant and shimmering waterfall. Some gleamed and sparkled with beads, crystals, and sequins. All were crafted with love and delicate care.

Perhaps I should note at this time that the ordinary observer peering down at the little glass globe would see almost none of this. No furniture. No stuffed animals. No sewing machine. No array of sparkling costumes. The ordinary observer would see only a solitary ballerina figure in a pale pink tutu, pirouetting in a fixed rotation. Undeniably a thing of beauty, but a mere shadow of the true beauty that resided within her. A beauty that only those blessed and cursed with a soul could see.

Likewise, the ordinary observer could not hear the true song of the music box. The casual eye could certainly appreciate the fine craftsmanship of the music box. It was gracefully carved and coated in gleaming black lacquer. Against the sheer, dark background, intricately painted cherry blossoms framed a great, glowing, red-orange firebird, wings splayed wide as it rose into the sky. This magnificent motif could be seen by all, yet the casual ear could hear but one simple, pleasant tune, repeated over and over until the box wound down and the dance ended. Only the broken-hearted could hear the secret refrain that brought the tiny ballerina to life and called her to the dance. And for a few fleeting moments, the enchantment of her dance brought the broken-hearted back to life.

Sometimes she danced to Turandot by Puccini. Sometimes she danced to Swan Lake or the Nutcracker by Tchaikovsky. Sometimes she danced to "Sukiyaki" by Kyu Sakamoto. Sometimes she danced to "River Flows in You" by Yiruma. Sometimes she danced to Nocturne in C-Sharp Minor by Chopin. Sometimes she danced to Winter from Vivaldi's the Four Seasons.

But always the dance was heartfelt and captivating. The tiny ballerina felt the music pierce into the depths of her heart and her soul. And it was from there that she danced. Such poignant grace and emotion cannot be described in mere words. Every part of the tiny ballerina's body moved and flowed to the music. Every gesture was a masterpiece, from the most dramatic leaps and spins to the slightest movement of a hand or the tilt of her head. She glided across the surface of the globe, body leaning backward, arms spread wide like outstretched wings. She pirouetted. She spun in breathtaking circles, back arched, hands reaching gracefully toward the heavens. She sprang lithely into the air, a single arm raised above her head, as she was wont to do. She soared. She flew. She clung to each note that chimed briefly in the air, fading, blending, dissolving into the melody. And like the song, the dance was at once ephemeral and eternal. It was almost too beautiful to bear.

The tiny ballerina put all that she had, all that she was, into the dance. All of her heart. All of her soul. And as the final notes died in the air, and the dance ended, she wept from her soul. And the broken-hearted felt their hearts break anew.

In the end, the tiny ballerina's dance, and her life, progressed much like Vivaldi's Four Seasons. She frolicked lightly through the carefree days of Spring. She gained strength, skill, and confidence as she leapt and pirouetted through Summer. She honed her skills and glided in glorious arcs and circles through the Fall. Then, at last, came the waning twilight of Winter with its cold gust, as it always does.

A different chime rang through the air. The chime of a clock that has struck midnight. The tiny ballerina stood cold and still as the dome of her glass globe rose into the dark sky and faded in the distance. She knew it was time.

With tears welling in her eyes, the tiny ballerina stepped forward and left the comfort of her home for the first time in her life. What lay beyond she did not know. She only hoped that there was something beautiful waiting for her in the outside world.

As she walked away, the tiny ballerina turned back to take one last glance at her old home. And there…

Inside the clear glass globe that was the only home she had ever known, a perfect tiny ballerina danced to the melancholy chimes of an exquisitely crafted music box.

The Prisoner and the Lion

Aaron A. A. Smith

There once was a prisoner who had been sealed behind his walls for so long that he could no longer remember his own name or face. For a while, his only sense of identity (such as it was) was attached to his prisoner identification number. But over time, that too faded from his memory.

The prisoner could no longer remember what crime, if any, he had committed. And he could not remember how long he had been behind his walls. It may have been years, or centuries, or forever. And in the end, what was the difference?

He could vaguely recall a time long ago when he still had some life and hope left inside him. In those days, he took every chance to bask in the bright light of day, following the sun as it made its daily journey across the confines of his enclosure. But over time, the prisoner began to shrink from the sun. He leaned against the walls and huddled against the cool, dark patches, moving from one shady alcove to the next as the garish orb in the sky pursued him around the yard. Sometimes he napped in the shadows.

Yet always, for as long as he could remember, when night fell he would stand in the same spot under the white, luminous moonlight and count the stars. He had a running total in his head.

Over time, the sun and the wind and the rain and time itself began to erode the prison walls. Cracks, crags, pores, fissures, rough jags, and other irregularities scarred its ancient surface.

At last on one night the prisoner cautiously examined the decaying face of the walls. As familiar as the face of a loved one, but changed and aged. He ran his fingers up and down the mottled surface of the wall, feeling the rough crevices and indentations. The wounds of time. He reached out and found a handhold. Then a foothold. And at long last, the prisoner climbed his wall and swung over the top to the other side.

He landed on a coal-gray cobblestone path in a narrow lane. He took a deep breath and turned around to take in his surroundings. Shops and homes lined the street. Little flower planters dangled from balconies, bursting in brilliant color beneath the moonlight. The king's castle loomed at the far end of the road. But the prisoner could not comprehend what any of these things were, or what they meant. All he knew of the world were the prison walls around him, the ground below, and the stars and sky above.

This unfamiliar world beyond his prison walls both intrigued and frightened the prisoner. His heart surged with the elation and relief of freedom. But it also raced with anxiety, confusion, and a vague yet overwhelming sense of dread.

Then the ominous clang of the castle bell pierced the calm quiet of the night. Trumpets blared. The king's watchmen shouted. The castle's drawbridge fell and the king's men emerged—spectral knights in dark armor, sitting astride dark steeds. The knights carried swords, lances, maces, and crossbows. Instinctively, the prisoner fled. The knights followed…

As the prisoner ran, he searched for any place to hide, any means of escape. Ahead he spotted a familiar, almost comforting feature—a wall. With the desperate energy of panic, he scaled the wall and pitched himself over the top. He landed in a crouch in a soft patch of dirt and grass. He stood up and tried to catch his breath.

A low rumble rose from the shadows behind the prisoner. A calculated chuffle. A knowing and eager growl of hunger. The prisoner turned around.

The lion stared at the man and the man stared at the lion. The man looked up at the sky to count the stars one last time. But from where he now stood, he could not get his bearings. He was standing under a different sky.

OUT OF FUEL

Erin Camille Jackson

The view of earth, from their little window, was distracting Jim from the seemingly endless chess game in which they found themselves engaged. But, there would be an end. However, neither of them knew quite when that would come. How long had they been out there, all alone? Jim tried to sneak a glance at the calendar. It was discretely tucked behind a large panel of once flashing lights and buttons.

"Nope. Don't look at that," George, Jim's lone companion, grumbled without even looking up from the magnetized chess board. They had rules about the confounded calendar. It was for the best, Jim knew. It could take over…and it had at first.

"I wasn't. I was just thinking, or something, I guess." Jim returned his focus to a ponderous trap facing his remaining bishop. He tried to let the blue and white orb retract to the tiny, scary prison cell in the back of his mind, where he could lock it up and just not look at it. This trick was becoming more and more difficult to execute. He rubbed his face, feeling the rather thick stubble that he'd let collect there.

A few days ago Jim and George had turned off all the "superfluous" power drains on the ship. The previously annoying, ever presence of the flashing lights was no longer an issue. They maintained the necessities, for now, as there was no longer a point to anything further. Those other systems were just reminders of the inevitable.

George had an incredible knack for finding tasks to fill his days, even with many of the ship's functions shut down. His favorite activity seemed to be tending to the many plants that they had brought along on their journey. He carefully investigated each leaf and frond. Most of these were air plants, but some had soil that required watering from the ship's supply. Luckily, the supply of water was able to be replenished by a strange device that turned the ever gathering ice crystals into useable irrigation. Another device filtered and recycled the men's urine. He loved watering and caring for the plants. The precious plants served to produce all-important oxygen, but Jim felt that George's obsession was something much more primordial. George loved the plants. Jim thought, often and sadly, that George could have had a beautiful life with a small farm as his only concern. He could have lived late into his years, surrounded by green things that he loved. Jim tried to push those kinds of fantasies into the locked cell of his mind, before they took on their tragically Grimm fairytale features. But, watching George fawn over his beloved plants made this quite difficult.

Jim had taken up sketching to fill the long, nearly silent hours. At first, he'd sketched the inside of their ship: the control panels, the spider web of wires above their heads, their grey bunks bolted to the wall. But that rapidly bored him. Each drawing felt bleaker than the one before. He stopped drawing the ship.

For George's birthday Jim drew him three drawings of the precious plants. It was better than drawing the mechanical home they shared. George was truly touched, much to Jim's amazement. George adhered the generous works of art to his bunk wall with great care and ceremony. Jim would occasionally notice George touching the delicately depicted biologicals as if they were treasured family portraits, instead of sketches by a worn out fellow space traveler.

After those plant drawings Jim allowed himself to draw the slowly fading view of Earth from their window. Initially, he only did this when George was otherwise occupied with his plants. But, eventually, it became a kind of compulsion. Jim's bunk wall was crammed, even impermeably collaged, with images of the receding planet. Almost imperceptibly, each image was shrinking as the incomprehensible void was expanding and taking over the page. Jim also touched these pictures before going to sleep. They only felt cold and flat in the dark. He'd roll over and turn his back to them as he closed his eyes to rest.

***

A little over a month ago Jim and George had launched their cramped two-man ship into orbit around the Earth. This was to be a three-week test run of the new compact ship, just to document the experience and design qualities/flaws of their vessel. They both had joked that it was a little like a vacation road trip.

"Just to get away from it all."

Most of the innovations employed in the new ship were only variations of pre-existing technology. Things like the plant to oxygen conversion system and the waste to water system, etc. were simply supposed to utilize less fuel and work more quickly, but were basically the same as on previous ships. However, a few other modifications were intended to totally revamp their predecessors. These included the primary oxygen provisions system and the fuel power mechanisms, which were the main focuses of Jim's and George's trip. If it went exceptionally well these changes would be applied to all future ships, changing the way space travel was conducted. Jim and George were lucky enough to be the very first to experience this revolutionary advance in their field.

***

Jim was resting in his bunk, but unable to find sleep. He was inclined to ponder the ponderousness of it all when the darkness refused to cradle his mind into dreams. In all actuality, he hated his dreams. They haunted him with rerunning movies of his life, or tortured him with plans he'd made for the eventual future. Neither was of any comfort to Jim. Without gentle sleep he gave in to flashes of what had happened.

He recalled a perfect Earth, centered in the window. He did not yet draw her. But that view of Earth had been precisely as it should be, to his eye. He'd turned to call George over, so that they might share this moment. As he turned away from the view he felt a gargantuan jolt. It knocked him back against his bunk like he'd been struck with a 100 MPH fastball. When he'd recovered his wits he'd found George slumped against the control panel, bleeding from a small cut to his forehead.

"George?" Jim rubbed his throbbing shoulder.

"Yeah…I'm good. Fine here." George gingerly touched his forehead to reassure himself. All seemed to be intact. Now they needed to investigate the ship.

Jim was already picking up the few broken items when George began checking the gauges. Nothing serious was broken. Mostly, things had just been knocked crooked. That was a relief. Maybe it had just been some kind of mechanical hiccup.

"I think it was just a bizarre power surge. So far things seem to be…" George trailed off. He stood, studying one of the many gauges. It seemed to be vexing him.

"What's up? Anything screwy?" Jim paused in his task of remaking his bunk. He seemed to have one illusive pillow. How could a damn pillow wander off on a tiny space ship? It made him think of the socks that always got eaten by his laundry machine at home.

"It's the fuel levels. I think that jolt was a power surge. We just rushed forward…apparently *way* forward, out into space. The fuel pump action must have forced out a massive expulsion of power." George sounded mechanical, almost metallic.

Jim replayed George's statement in his head to see if he'd understood. The pillow was peeking out from under the bunk, next to a sock he'd been puzzling about earlier that week. George turned to face Jim. His face was distorted into the pale image of one about to meet the Inquisition or the gallows. It had a blankness covering something not quite believed. It read, "This is not true. This is not where I am."

"The surge blew nearly all of our fuel." George found his words.

While that notion sank in on Jim, George followed up with yet another morsel of disturbing information.

"Jim, it also pushed us so far that…that we're out of orbit. We're out of orbit."

Jim digested these statements for a moment.

"So, we're running out of fuel and drifting out into space." He sat down next to George.

"Yes." George stared at his hands. George's hands had a half moon of dirt under his nails from tending his plants. The farmer.

"Slowly, the oxygen system will fail and the other electrical systems will, even before that. The plants aren't enough to really help. We are drifting to nowhere."

"Until we are nowhere. Nothing." Jim thought out loud.

"Yes."

Outside the little window the blue orb of planet Earth already seemed to be receding into the distance. It was currently becoming their past. A place and time that had been. Ahead, the expanse of deepest black space loomed as whatever future remained.

***

So, there they sat, in their metal floating castle, as it drifted ever further into the empty. They had their routine and their distractions. But, mostly they had vacant lapses of time. The inevitable can become just another fact of the day, like eating or sleeping. They waited without waiting.

Jim's drawings lost their detail, but he continued to draw. It was as if by rendering her image he kept Earth alive for them. Alive, but gone and as good as imaginary now.

George tended his sacred plants. A space farmer on a lost plantation. He had little else to do once they'd shut down most of the systems. It felt a bit like pulling the plug on a brain dead loved one. Of course the plug was essentially pulled already.

They played chess and rarely spoke. Neither of them could figure out what to say. There was silence. There was darkness. And they were living in an encapsulated world, until the time came when they would cease to be, as their little world floated on without its inhabitants.

Room 7

Aaron A. A. Smith

The faded blue-gray paint on the steps of the hotel was chipping, flaking, and peeling. Dolan cleared them in one casual leap, grabbed the scratched metal handle of the glass front door, and let himself in. He swaggered into what couldn't really be called a lobby—a check-in/check-out desk on the left, a couple of vending machines hunched in the shadow of a staircase on the right.

A clanging thump issued from one of the vending machines. Dolan stopped and cast a sidelong glance in the direction of the sound. Somehow the New York Yankees cap pulled low above his eyes gave him the air of an Old West gunslinger.

A t-girl prostitute was fishing a can of Diet Pepsi out of the soda machine. Her eyes darted furtively to where Dolan stood, registering his presence, but assiduously avoiding direct eye contact. Dolan did the same. The t-girl snatched her soda from the machine and marched up the stairs, high heels echoing through the hall.

Dolan sauntered past the night front desk clerk, a nice middle-aged Chinese man whose difficulty with the English language—combined with Dolan's unfamiliarity with the subtleties of Cantonese—had made Dolan's check-in something of a challenge. The clerk nodded politely, keeping his gaze slightly down, avoiding Dolan's face. Dolan returned the gesture.

Dolan had known plenty of places like this back in the good old days in New York. Shady places. Places to score. Places to whore. Places to shoot up and pass out on the floor. Every room a cubicle of illicit activity and vice. And sometimes worse. And always in places like this, no one looked you dead in the face. No one looked you directly in the eye. And you did the same for them. It was a common courtesy in the shadow world. Nobody saw nothin.'

Beyond the night desk stretched a narrow hallway. White hotel room doors framed by imperial red walls. Dolan walked a few paces down the hall, then faced left. He stared at the door to his room. Number 7. The same as the number on the back of his gray New York Yankees road jersey.

Dolan fished his room key out of his front jeans pocket and slipped it into the lock of the scratched and fading brass-colored door handle. The old handle wobbled loosely in his grip. He entered the room, shut the door, and flipped on the light switch. The bulb of a lamp flickered to life.

A man was sitting at the little circular table across from Dolan's bed, gun in hand. A half-drunk bottle of Jameson occupied the center of the table like a votive offering at the world's laziest voodoo altar. The dim lamplight cast a half-shadow over the man's face. He leveled the barrel of his gun at Dolan's chest and smiled.

"Hello, Dolan," the man said. "Been a long time."

"Hello, Sweeney," Dolan nodded in acknowledgement. "It has."

"But I always knew this day would come," Sweeney said. "And so did you."

Dolan cocked his head and shrugged.

"You packin'?" Sweeney asked.

"Nope."

"You'll understand if I don't trust you. You know the drill, Dolan."

Dolan turned around and put his hands up over his head. Sweeney stood and patted Dolan down. When he was satisfied that Dolan was unarmed, Sweeney dragged his chair across the floor and set it beside the table. He sat down, gun barrel still leveled at Dolan. "Ok, Dolan," he said. "Go ahead and have a seat on the bed over there." He gestured toward the bed with his gun.

Dolan turned and took a step toward the bed, then stopped dead in his tracks. There was a Los Angeles Dodgers hat on the bed.

"Oh, what the fuck, Sween?" Dolan winced.

Sweeney burst into laughter, and in that instant Dolan heard the same mischievous giggle that had belonged to his childhood best friend.

"If you're gonna shoot me, just shoot me," Dolan said. "But not in the presence of Dodgers memorabilia."

This made Sweeney laugh even harder. Dolan couldn't help but join in. And for a brief moment, they ceased to be the two hardened men they had become. Men who had committed crimes. Men who had killed. Men who were even now planning to kill. In that moment, they were the echoes of two little boys who had once played together in the streets and parks of The City.

Then the laughter trailed off and the two men continued with the inevitable.

Dolan sat down on the edge of the bed, a faint smirk still playing at the corners of his mouth. The old springs in the mattress groaned under his weight. Sweeney was sitting directly across from Dolan at the chincy round hotel table.

His finger rested casually against the trigger of his gun. A faded circular scar on the back of his hand glinted in the lamplight.

"You know a hat on a bed is bad juju, Sween," Dolan said.

"So they say."

"And a Dodgers hat to boot."

"'Dem bums," Sweeney shook his head. "Double juju."

"Get this damn thing out of my sight," Dolan said as he flipped the hat to Sweeney. Sweeney caught the hat with his left hand and tossed it under his chair in one fluid motion.

"Hey, hey," said Dolan. "Looks like we've still got the old 6-4-3 double play moves after all."

"We should," Sweeney said. "We practiced it like a million times in high school."

"We did." Dolan raised an eyebrow. "Good times."

Sweeney nodded. "The best."

The men paused for a moment, lost in nostalgia. Then they shook themselves from their reverie once more.

"I don't know about all that hat on the bed mumbo jumbo," Sweeney said, "but I'm a little bit concerned about that fruity teddy bear you've got over there." He lifted his chin in the direction of a round, pillow-sized cream and tan-colored stuffed panda that peered adorably upward with big saucer eyes. "What the fuck's up with that?"

"Oh, her?" Dolan said. He patted the panda twice on the head. "That's just Mama Panda. She's completely harmless. Here, why don't you give her a little pet?" Dolan wrapped a hand under the panda's belly, as if preparing to hand her to Sweeney.

"Nuh-uh." Sweeney shook his head and recoiled in his seat.

"Suit yourself." Dolan grinned, enjoying his old friend's discomfort. "What's a matter, Sween? You think she's gonna bite? Make you light in the loafers? Turn you into a Japanese schoolgirl?"

"Can't be too careful," Sweeney said gravely. He didn't seem to catch the joke.

"Guess not." Dolan tilted his head in an "oh, well" kind of shrug. "But, anyway—since you asked—Mama Panda is my trusty, indispensable travel companion."

Sweeney stared blankly, confused.

"Look," Dolan said. "You know how shitty little hotels like this give you shitty pillows that don't support your neck?"

Sweeney nodded emphatically. "Yeah, that's true," he said with all the bemused enthusiasm of a child who had just had an epiphany.

"Right," Dolan continued. "So these cheap-ass hotel pillows kept giving me a crick in my neck."

"Yeah, I hate that," Sweeney interjected, rubbing the back of his neck with his free hand.

"So you know what I mean," Dolan said. "Anyway, I must have tried a dozen different travel pillows over the years, but none of them worked. I just kept waking up with that damn crick in my neck.

"Then, finally, about nine years ago, I'm in Hong Kong. And I'm walking back to my hotel from this little whorehouse

I knew, and my neck is killing me. So I'm going past all these neon lights and dumpling shops and storefronts when I just stop in front of this store window. I don't even know why. But there I am, rubbing my stiff neck and looking in through this store window. Turns out it's some kind of novelty shop or a souvenir store or something like that. And there are all these toys and gadgets and stuffed animals everywhere. And there she was." Dolan tapped Mama Panda twice on the head. "So I'm standing there rubbing my neck when something occurs to me—this panda is about the right size and shape to fit into that spot between my neck and head. At this point I'm pretty desperate. I'd have tried about anything. So I figured I'd give her a shot. I walked in, bought her, took her back to the hotel, and used her as a pillow. Haven't had a crick in my neck since. Turns out this panda here is ergonomically designed to fit the contours of the human neck." Dolan extended a hand, palm up, toward Mama Panda.

Sweeney knit his brows and rubbed his temple with the first two fingers of his left hand. He smiled and shook his head. Then he burst out laughing. "Man, Dolan," he said, leaning back in his chair, "you ain't changed a bit. Ergonomic teddy bears. Goofy-ass stories. You always were a funny one. I kinda missed that."

"Yeah," Dolan nodded and leaned forward, elbows resting on his knees, hands pressed loosely together.

Both men's eyes softened and took on a faraway look. They weren't looking at anything in the room. They weren't even looking at the present. They were looking at the past.

"But I'm calling bullshit on that Hong Kong panda story," Sweeney said, pointing the index finger of his non-gun hand at Dolan and grinning a sideways grin.

Dolan sat up straight, spread his palms wide, and shrugged. "Well, there is a panda, she is from Hong Kong, and there is a story." Now both of the old gangsters burst into laughter.

Sweeney glanced at the bottle of Jameson. He pinged it with his finger. "Still drinking the good stuff, I see."

Dolan nodded.

"Jame-O always was my favorite," Sweeney said. "Man, we drank our fair share of it together back in high school. Though I always thought you were more of a Scotch man."

"They had a sale on Jame-O at the Ralph's on Sunset. Can't pass up a good bargain on whiskey."

"I might have to swing by later and pick up a couple bottles."

"You should."

"Remember when you used to sneak this shit to school in your old man's flask and we'd drink it behind the gym?"

Dolan chuckled. "I do."

Sweeney grabbed a couple of cheap plastic hotel cups and slid them to the center of the table next to the whiskey. He picked up the bottle and sloshed it. "One for old times?"

Dolan shrugged. "Why not?"

Sweeney unscrewed the bottle and poured two cups with his free hand. He leaned forward and handed a cup to Dolan.

Sweeney raised his plastic hotel cup of Jameson.

"Slainte," he toasted.

"Slainte," Dolan answered, raising his cup in return.

The men each took a healthy first swig of whiskey, then settled back to savor the rest. Dolan took a second swig, then stretched out casually on the bed, head resting on Mama Panda, one hand beneath her fluffy belly, the other balancing his whiskey cup on his stomach.

"You and that bear, man." Sweeney grinned and shook his head again. "You always were an odd cat, and you just didn't give a fuck. You know, I always thought that was cool. Odd cat," he repeated slowly, still shaking his head. He straightened up in his seat and took another sip of whiskey. "Honestly, I never did quite get you. But I always did know you. That's how I knew I'd find you here. I knew if the Yankees made it back to the Series, you'd show up. You just wouldn't be able to stay away.

"Mind you, it's no easy thing finding a man who don't want to be found in a crowd of fifty-thousand people," Sweeney continued, a smug, self-satisfied tone entering his voice. "I had to grease a lot of palms, break some kneecaps, put in a lot of frequent-flyer miles between New York and L.A. But I knew I'd find you."

Sweeney smirked for a moment in petty triumph, then his face fell. "You had to know I'd be here looking for you." A twinge of sadness colored his words. Regret. Confusion. "So why take the risk? Why not lay low, drink a couple beers, and watch on TV? You could have just stayed disappeared. So why?"

Dolan was silent for a while. Then he sat up and took a sip of whiskey. "Because it's baseball," he said. "Because it's my team. Because there's nothing like being there at the ballpark to see your team play in the World Series, and I couldn't give that up for anything. Because baseball is the only sport with a soul. Well, except for figure skating, but I'm pretty sure you don't want to hear about that."

"Not really." Sweeney stiffened. He took another slug of Jame-O. Dolan followed suit.

"Because it's history," Dolan continued. "It's the Yankees against the Dodgers. Just like it used to be."

"Same World Series matchup as the year you were born, right Dolan?" Sweeney asked.

"It is," Dolan answered.

"And the same matchup on the year you're going out."

"Worse things than going out on a classic matchup. It's actually sort of comforting. There's something poetic about it. Just the symmetry of it. Sort of like Mark Twain coming into the world and going out of it with Halley's Comet."

Sweeney squinted at Dolan. "There you go gettin' all deep like you always used to. That I don't miss."

Dolan shrugged. "It's not to everyone's taste." He took another swig of whiskey.

"But this shit is," Sweeney said, holding up his cup of whiskey. He took a slug.

"Or at least it should be," Dolan said and knocked back another quick gulp of Jame-O. "I'm highly suspicious of any man who doesn't drink whiskey."

"I hear that. Those assholes are either on the program or they drink tequila."

"Ugh!" Dolan grimaced. "I'm not sure which is worse.

The two childhood friends laughed once more, then fell silent.

"Why, Dolan?" Sweeney finally asked, sadness returning to his voice. Only now it was more than just a twinge. He seemed to be staring into the distance at nothing in particular.

"Why what, Sween? The baseball thing again?"

"No, not that goddammit!" Sweeney held up his bullet-scarred right hand. The barrel of his gun pointed up toward the ceiling. "Why?" he repeated.

"You know why. At least the big part. You were going to kill that boy."

"He saw our faces! He could have made us!" Sweeney took a breath. Lowered his head. "It shouldn't have gone down like that."

"No, it shouldn't have," Dolan agreed. "A lot of things shouldn't have gone down the way they did. That piece of shit dealer shouldn't have had a party the night before a deal that size. That junkie broad shouldn't have brought her kid to a party like that. She shouldn't have taken too much shit and ODed in the night. That dumbass dealer shouldn't have been short on product because he'd been passing it out as party favors. He shouldn't have pulled on us. And you shouldn't have pulled on that kid. He was, what, ten maybe? Maybe?"

Dolan ran his fingers across his chin. He breathed out. "But it ain't much good thinkin' about all the things that should or shouldn't have been. It's just one thing after the other. It becomes this bottomless pit that just sinks down and down forever."

"Jesus," Sweeney gasped, inching back in his chair. "I wish you hadn't said that."

"But you're right, Sween," Dolan said. "Things shouldn't have been the way they were. They should never have been the way they were."

"What are you talking about?" Sweeney asked.

"I never should have brought you into this life. You were my best friend. Like a little brother. Like some puppy following at my heels. But there was always a rabid dog under the surface. I saw it. The old man saw it. And I guess that's the real reason I brought you into the family. Not so much because you were my friend, though that was part of it. But if I had been a good friend, I would never have let you into the crew. I would have let you live your own life. But instead, I brought you into crime and death. I fed that rabid dog inside you and helped create the infamous Mad Dog Sweeney. And for that, I'm sorry."

A shadow passed over Sweeney's face, part regretful, part angry, part sad. After a long pause, he said, "Dolan, you said there was another reason why you did what you did. Besides the kid…"

Dolan straightened up and looked Sweeney in the eye. “Because I had to get away,” he said. “I couldn’t do it anymore. I just—had to get away.”

Sweeney slumped his shoulders. “You almost did.”

“Almost,” Dolan said, raising his cup of whiskey. Sweeney returned the salute.

“Slainte!”

“Slainte!”

Dolan and Sweeney gulped down the last of the whiskey in their cheap plastic cups.

“One for the road?” Dolan raised an eyebrow.

“Why not,” Sweeney answered with a faint smile that never reached his eyes.

Dolan handed Sweeney his empty plastic cup, then laid back down on the bed, head resting on Mama Panda, hands crossed under her belly like a child lying back in a field and gazing at the stars in a tranquil night sky. A thing he had never done.

Sweeney poured the final round of whiskey. He reached out his left hand to pass Dolan his cup.

From beneath Mama Panda, Dolan drew a pistol. Two sharp chirps from a silencer pierced the room as Dolan squeezed off two rounds into Sweeney's chest. Sweeney fell back in his chair, gasping for breath. The cup of whiskey fell to the floor.

Dolan stood up. "I'm sorry, Sweeney. I truly am." He pointed the gun between Sweeney's eyes. Dolan pulled the trigger.

Dolan snatched up his suitcase, whiskey bottle, and Mama Panda and hurried out of room number 7. As he closed the door, he saw the barrel of a pistol in his periphery. It was pointed at his head.

The gun lowered.

"It's ok, kid," Dolan said. "It's over. All of it. No more running. No more looking over our shoulders. We're in the clear."

The young man in the New York Yankees hat and gray Yankees road jersey stuffed his pistol into the duffel bag that was slung over his shoulder. He exhaled. “Really?”

“Really, kid.”

“Now what?”

“Well, now how about we get something to eat and check into the Roosevelt?”

“Yeah?”

Dolan nodded. “Yep. And tomorrow we’ve got game seven. I’m feeling lucky, all things considered. Time to beat L.A.”

“Let’s go Yankees,” said the kid. “Beat L.A.!”

Dolan put his arm around the kid’s shoulder, and number 7 and number 99 walked out into the warm Hollywood night.

La Chatte Grise

Aaron A. A. Smith

I had been on her tail for days. Following leads. Asking around. Greasing palms. Breaking legs. Wandering through every back alley and seedy gin joint in town. Searching. Waiting… But still no dice. I guess that's just how it goes for a shamus like me.

Then finally I got a tip. The source was disreputable. But usually reliable.

I walked down the dirty city streets through patches of lamplight and shadow. I lowered the brim of my Fedora and pulled up the collar of my trench coat, dodging staggering hobos all the way. I trudged with steady purpose beneath the dim acetylene glare, following the trolley tracks west down Cats Street. It didn't matter which side of the tracks I was following. Down here, all sides of the tracks are the wrong side of the tracks.

Up ahead on the right, I saw an open black double-doorway. Above, scrawled in faded white paint on a chipping black brick wall was an outline sketch of a cat. A sign at the cat's feet read "La Chatte Noire." Just where Behemoth had said it would be. He had been good. I made a mental note to bring him some salmon treats.

As I approached the doorway, faint fragments of light splintered through a half-drawn black velvet curtain that hung at the entrance. The muffled sounds of a live band reverberated out into the street. Bass vibrating through the walls, past the curtains, through the sidewalk into my spats.

I pulled back the curtains, trying not to think about what sorts of germs and diseases might have been clinging to that old velvet rag.

I stepped inside and took in my surroundings. The gin joint was dim and dank. Stale. A wisping tail of cigarette smoke swirled in the half-light like dissipating vapors of dragon breath. Strings of white Christmas lights and neon beer signs brought faint glows of illumination to the lounge.

And ambience. I guess. Can't forget about ambience. Two rows of horseshoe-shaped red leather booths ran the length of the room. From a tiny, ramshackle stage against the back wall, a jazz quintet played a cover of "Maneater" by Hall & Oates. Not a bad rendition, I thought.

I scanned the room, looking for possible threats: coppers, high-ranking gangsters, gun thugs, etc. And looking for her. Nothing much to see at first. Just a bunch of two-bit mugs in polyester. And a real tomato of a cocktail waitress in a short tight black dress. Her gams went all the way up to her neck.

The cocktail waitress walked over to the booth nearest the band and set a shot glass of milk down on the table. And there she was—the target. Little Miss J, AKA the Goblin. Finally. Yeah, Behemoth was definitely due some salmon treats.

Miss J gave the cocktail waitress a dirty look, then swatted the glass of milk off the table. She cocked her head. "Meow!" she snarled. Real demanding and judgmental-like.

"Oopsie!" squeaked the waitress. "Did you spill your drinkie?"

Miss J made no reply. She just stared daggers at the waitress.

I slid into the booth and sat down across from Miss J. She turned her head to glance at me and froze. Her eyes went wide, then froze like the rest of her. She knew she had been naughty.

"Nice gams," I said to the cocktail waitress. "The milk's on me."

"Thanks, handsome," she said, smiling. Just a little. At the corners of her mouth and right at the top of her cheeks just below her eyes. She tilted her head and raised one shoulder. "And what can I get you, sweetie?"

"Canadian Club. Neat," I said.

"Ooh, nice choice." She wiped up the spilled milk on the table and picked up the downed shot glass, never looking away from my face.

Miss J looked at me plaintively. She meowed twice and rocked back and forth on her front paws.

"What, you want one, too?" I scoffed. Miss J nodded twice and rocked on her front paws again. Emphatically.

I shrugged. "Two whiskeys, I guess," I said to the waitress.

"Oh my God, you two are so adorable," she squealed.

"Yes," I said. "Yes we are." I flashed a smile and narrowed my eyes just a bit. The cocktail waitress' smile widened. She bit her bottom lip and cocked her head. She blushed. At least one of those whiskeys was going to be on the house.

"Ok," the waitress giggled. "I'll be back with your drinks in two shakes." She wiggled her hips twice in a pantomime tail wag. Then she extended her arm to full length and pointed her index finger at me. "Don't go anywhere."

"We'll be right here, sweetheart," I said.

The cocktail waitress took one dainty yet awkward step back, tucked in one shoulder, and turned and walked back to the bar. She looked back at me over her shoulder three times on the way.

Miss J squinted and shook her head disapprovingly. “Meow,” she snorted.

“Cut the crap,” I said. “I know cats can talk. Some of my best confidential informants are cats. Great at covert work. Naturally sneaky.”

Miss J inhaled sharply. I always get a kick out of seeing a cat get all offended.

“As opposed to hoomans?” she retorted.

“Touche’,” I allowed, tipping my Fedora. I had to laugh.

The cocktail waitress returned to the table and set down the whiskeys. “There you go, sweeties,” she said. “I just can’t get over how cute the two of you are. Miss kitty, did you say something funny?”

Miss J stared daggers at the waitress again.

“Yeah, she’s a regular riot,” I said. “She was just telling me a real corker of a joke about how this shamus, a cat, and a cocktail waitress walk into a bar.”

"I've never heard it." A dimwitted curiosity rose in her voice.

"Nevermind," I said. "It's kind of a long one."

"Oooh," she nodded. "Maybe later then."

"Maybe," I said. "What do you think, Miss Kitty? Would you like to tell the nice lady a joke later?"

The waitress leaned down toward Miss J. "Oh yes, Miss Kitty, would you like to tell me a jokey wokey?" She reached out a hand to pet Miss J. Miss J swatted the encroaching hand away.

"Oh, goodness!" The waitress retracted her hand.

"See what I mean?" I said to the waitress. "This one's a laugh a minute. A bit touchy, though."

"Is you cwanky?" the cocktail waitress cooed at Miss J. Miss J narrowed her eyes down to furious little slits.

"She is," I said, looking sidelong at Ms. J with a crooked grin. I was speaking to her, not to the waitress. Ms. J was aware of the fact. The waitress was not.

The fur down the middle of Ms. J's back stood up on end. She reminded me of a Rhodesian Ridgeback.

"Anything else I can get you two right now?" the cocktail waitress asked.

"Not at the moment, sweetheart," I answered.

"Ok then, handsome," she said. "I'll be back to check on you in a few." She smiled, tilted her head, and pointed a finger at me. Then she turned half way around, peeked over her shoulder, and said: "And by the way, the drinks are on me."

"Thanks, kid," I said. "You're a real doll."

The waitress rolled her shoulder in that same flirty, pretend coy pose. She tilted her head again. Giggled like a schoolgirl. Blushed. Then she turned and walked back to the bar, peeking back at me over her shoulder every few steps.

The cat was glaring at me. "I hate you, hooman," she said. "You are not funny. And stop playing with that damn chatterbox."

"Is you cwanky," I teased.

"Shut up, hooman. Still not funny. You know damn well that cats hate that condescending baby talk. We are your superiors. Hoomans wait on us hand and foot. Feed us. Clean our poo and steal it. The ancient Egyptians knew our divine status."

I took a sip of whiskey. "Maybe," I said. "But you know hoomans like me, ones who know that cats can talk, don't much care for that 'meow' crap. Easier for everyone if you just say what's on your mind." I took another swig of the old brown. "So what gives? Why the whole meow act?"

"Just for kicks," she said.

"Really? All that bother. Not being able to just say what you want. Just for some kind of gag?"

"Yes." She lifted her chin.

"That's it? A joke?"

"Yes. Most hoomans very stupid. We trick them. 'Meow, meow, meow!' They try to figure out our language. Run around in circles like fools. Is all a big joke on the hoomans. Very funny." The corners of her mouth turned up. She almost seemed to laugh.

The jazz band finished their cover of "Maneater." I took another swig of whiskey. Ms. J shifted her weight back and forth on her front paws. She eagerly thumped her tail twice on the seat of the booth. It was a short fluffy snub-tail just a few inches long.

Ms. J narrowed her eyes: a blinking cat version of batting her eyelashes. "Give me some whiskey, hooman."

Miss J. glanced over at the jazz band leader. He nodded at the cat and tipped the brim of his Fedora. The band struck up a tune. An instrumental version of "Memory" from *Cats.* Something about that song always makes me feel downright blue. It reminds me how ephemeral everything is. How temporary. Time passes. You can't do anything to stop it. Everything beautiful fades away and is one day lost. Even the memory fades. For some reason the song made me think of a tiny ballerina in a glass globe, spinning in a perfect and beautiful arc.

"Meow!" The agitated cry of my companion snapped me out of my reverie.

"Hooman, wake up."

I took a breath. And a healthy swig of my whiskey.

"You were a million miles away, hooman. Sad hooman. Very sad. I can see it in your eyes. I smells it on you. No get lost in the dark place. Sometimes hoomans never get out."

I gulped down some more whiskey and had a coughing fit that had nothing to do with my drink.

Then the cat surprised me. She leapt across the booth and frantically rubbed her head against my leg. "No dying, hooman. Now you give me whiskey." Cat linear logic. Totally nonsequitur.

"You have a glass," I said.

"That's not how it works. Finish yours. It's low anyway."

I shrugged and drained my glass.

"Now," she continued. "Take my glass." I reached out and took her glass. "Now, very carefully and precisely put some whiskey in your mouth and stick your pinky finger in dere."

"What? Why?" Her instructions sounded bananas to me.

"Just do it, hooman."

I shrugged and did as the cat asked.

"Now," she said, "hold your finger out in front of my face."

Again I did as asked. The cat stuck out her tongue and lapped up the whiskey from my finger. She pulled her ears close to her head. Her eyes went wild and crazed. One of her front teeth snaggled outside of her mouth. It was drunk, loopy, cat addict face.

"You know," I said as we continued our new drinking routine, "Mr. Fuzzy Pants has every shamus and gumshoe in town looking for you. Lucky for you that I'm the one who found you first. I'll still have to bring you in, mind you. That was a mighty expensive shipment of catnip you heisted from Mr. Fuzzy pants. And he runs the underworld around here."

"Well," Ms. J said, licking whiskey off her fur, "somebody had to get that junk off the street. It was cut with something bad. Kept giving all the users hairballs."

"Don't play innocent with me, Ms. J. I know you've been dealing that nip on the streets and in the kennels. And using a bit yourself."

"Every girl is entitled to one or two teeny little vices, isn't she? And I don't own a hooman. A kitty's gotta eat, after all."

"Tell it to Mr. Fuzzy pants," I said.

"You wouldn't! You couldn't!" Ms. J gasped.

"Come on, sweetheart. It's about time to go."

"No!" the cat pouted. "I'm not moving."

I opened the breast of my trench coat, revealing a neon green spray bottle. "Don't make me use this thing," I said low under my breath."

"No!" she meowed.

"I'll call you a bad kitty," I threatened.

"You wouldn't."

"Last chance," I warned.

Ms. J hunkered down in the booth and stared me in the eye. "No."

"Bad kitty!" I hissed.

"Oh, hooman." The cat closed her eyes and turned her face away. "How could you be so cruel?" She slumped her shoulders and shook her head. "Fine. We go now. I takes you to the nip."

"Nice kitty," I said. I gulped down the last of the whiskey, gave her a lick off my finger, and scratched the top of her head between her ears.

***

Twenty minutes later we arrived at a big sterile-looking gray stone bank. The kind of building you see in old photos of Berlin at the height of the Third Reich.

"This is it?" I asked.

The cat, who had been tucked snugly under my left arm as I walked the derelict city blocks, peered up at me from under my coat lapel. She nodded. "This is it, hooman."

"Kinda late for a bank to be open."

"It is always open. To cats, anyway."

"Why is that?"

"Because this bank exists in two worlds: the everyday hooman world and the other world beyond. Is same with cats. We has two paws in this world, two in the other. Is why we are good witches' familiars, how we steals hooman breaths while they're sleeping, why we bites the feets—"

"What?"

"Nothing." She stared at me with wide-open frozen eyes. Then she looked up and away to the left.

I shrugged my shoulders, climbed the Third Reich bank steps, and swung open the smudged glass doors. A wave of bright, antiseptic light flooded my senses as I entered. The kind of light you might expect to see in Heaven, if Heaven were the waiting room of a dentist's office. The lobby was of a modest size, at least in terms of square-footage. But the domed ceiling reached high above, arching into its own artificial sky like a National Socialist *Oculus Dei.* Again the cold gray Third Reich architecture. Sterile, sterile, sterile. It might have been beautiful if it weren't so damn ugly.

"That way, hooman." The cat twitched her head toward a room on the right.

I walked into the room, cat still tucked snugly under my arm. The room was filled wall-to-wall with safety deposit boxes and nothing else. Every inch of every wall was lined with the things. Safety deposit boxes all the way down.

"It's in box number eighty-two about half way down on the left wall," the cat said. "But stay away from the alcove all the way in the back." Ms. J shuddered.

"Why?"

"It holds the safety posit box."

"This whole room is full of safety deposit boxes."

"No, hooman, the safety *posit* box." She enunciated the words precisely.

"What the hell is that?"

"Damn it, do hoomans know nothing?" she snorted. "It's a terrifying repository of arcane knowledge. Ideas, expositions. Philosophical, theological, and literary wisdom. Truth, falsehood. Sublimity and madness. All just squeezed in dere like a Pandora's Box of crazy. No go dere, hooman. Dat box full of infinite and infinitesimal ideas. Ideas themselves. Just sitting. Waiting. Growing. Like living things der own self."

"Jesus," I exhaled.

The kitty cocked her head at me. A kitty smile seemed to play at the corners of her kitty mouth. A little snaggle-tooth protruded over her lip.

I crossed the room and walked up to Ms. J's safety deposit box: a tall broad container with a metal front, just a bit smaller than a high school locker.

"Take the key," Ms. J said. "It's on a chain around my neck. Right next to a lock with the letter 'R' on it."

I felt for the key, unfastened it from the chain, scratched the kitty under the chin. She lifted up her chin and purred in response.

I slid the key into the lock and opened the box. Inside was a large gray plastic bag. I picked it up and looked inside. I grinned. The bag was stuffed to the seams with catnip.

"Who's a naught kitty?" I said.

***

We walked the dozen or so blocks back to my apartment, got into my black Studebaker, and headed to the grocery store. We avoided the hobos on the street, in the grocery store parking lot, in the aisles of the store itself. A horde of staggering, brown-bag winos… And worse.

We made a quick job of it. Picked up some cat food and treats, a litter box and kitty-litter, and a big brown plastic jug of Canadian Club.

When we got back to my flat, I fumbled in my coat pocket for the door key. I fished out the key and concentrated real hard on lining it up with the lock, but my hand kept shaking. I hadn't had enough to drink that night. I took a breath, steadied my hand, and managed to slip the key into the lock. The fit was a bit too tight, so I had to wriggle the key around and force it into the lock. With a bit of effort, the key turned and the lock clicked open.

The inside of my apartment is pretty nondescript. About what you'd expect from a low-key, hard-drinking, misanthropic shamus like me. Basic furniture, mostly in black. Couch. Desk with a green lamp. Old TV with rabbit ears. Bedroom. Bathroom.

The only items in my apartment of any note are my books and my rug. I collect books. Generally nothing expensive. No rare collector's items. But I kinda hoard the things. I've got lots of hardboiled detective novels, of course. Some Raymond Chandler. Some Dashiel Hammet. Plus some Haruki Murakami. Some Elmore Leonard. Some George V. Higgins. But the heart of my library is the history section. Especially the stuff about the classical world. The ancient Greeks and Romans. Herodotus and Thucydides. Caesar and

Xenophon. Arrian and Tacitus. The complete, unabridged Decline and Fall of the Roman Empire by Edward Gibbon. That's one of my favorites.

As for the rug, it's an old Oriental hand-woven piece. The real deal. I picked it up in a market in Tangiers. Don't ask me what I was doing there. It was work-related. Mostly. Anyway, it's a damn fine rug. Deep red background with some cream-colored geometric flower shapes that I'm sure have some deeper metaphoric or symbolic meaning I don't really understand. They kinda remind me of a Venus Flytrap, or that plant from *Little Shop of Horrors* that ate people. Especially when I'm a little tight and stare at it too long. But, as I was saying, it's a damn fine rug.

I flipped on the lights and deposited the kitty on the floor. Then I went to the kitchen and poured a glass of whiskey. The cat followed me every step, weaving between my ankles and nearly tripping me in her oblivious cat affection.

I took the whiskey glass in one hand and the bottle in the other, and crossed the living room to the couch. I sat with a tired grunt and reached for the TV remote. I pressed the power button, toggled the guide, and sipped at my whiskey. According to the guide, *Casablanca* was on. I toggled to the appropriate channel and hit the enter button. Bogey greeted me with his characteristic tough-guy swagger and one-of-a-kind way of talking. Yet there was something haunted and vulnerable about his performance in *Casablanca.* Something broken. "Of all the gin joints in all the world… Play it, Sam. If she can stand it, I can."

I leaned back and swigged some more whiskey. The cat jumped up onto the arm of the couch with that crazed "kitty wants a whiskey" glare clouding her eyes. She rocked back and forth on her front paws.

"More whiskey, hooman" she said.

I gave her a few finger licks of whiskey, then she settled next to me on the couch and we watched the movie together. At some point, I dozed off. And at some point the cat woke me up by loudly hacking up a hairball on my Oriental rug.

My head still murky with whiskey and sleep, I sat bolt-upright and tried to focus my eyes. They didn't care much for what they saw. Ms. J had gotten into the bag of catnip. Big piles of the stuff were strewn across the floor, and a big nip-laced hairball lay in front of Ms. J's feet, soiling my prized Oriental rug.

Ms. J froze. She peered up at me with that wide-eyed, guilty "oh shit" look that cats give you when you catch them red-handed being a bad kitty.

She moved her paws in front of the hairball, as if to conceal her crime. "Nothing," she said.

"Really?" I protested. "And on the rug?" I shook my head and pointed a finger at the cat. "Bad kitty!"

Ms. J hung her head in shame. "I is sorry, hooman. The nip has too much of a hold on me. I cans not resist it. I are poisoned by it. Just like so many other kitties. And more every day with that nip flooding the streets. It is pitiful, hooman. Pitiful."

I stood up. Scratched my head. Ran a hand down my face in consternation.

"Alright," I said. "I'm going to take care of this. But first I'm cleaning this rug."

***

I pulled my Studebaker up to the heavy iron gates. Beyond, at the end of a long gray cobbled drive, I spied Mr. Fuzzy Pants' mansion. It was one of those sprawling old California numbers. More big, gaudy, and lavish than tasteful. It looked like the sort of monstrosity that the illegitimate love child of Scrooge McDuck and William Randolph Hearst might commission.

The Studebaker's engine purred as it idled at the gate. I glanced over at the cardboard cat-carrier on the seat beside me.

"You sure you're up for this?" I asked Ms. J.

"I wouldn't miss this for all the nip in Hong Kong," she said. She huddled in the shadows of the kitty-carrier like a big round ball. Ready to pounce.

"Ok," I nodded.

I pressed the intercom button beside the gate. A singsong "meow" greeted me through the speaker. Mr. Fuzzy pants' catservant Mr. Jingles.

"Cut the shenanigans, Jeeves," I grumbled. He always hated that old Jeeves crack.

"Do you have an appointment to see Mr. Fuzzy Pants, sir?" he said in his obsequious yet self-satisfied tone.

"Better, old Jeevsey, I've got that missing shipment of cat nip. And the culprit who lifted it."

A long pause, then: "Really?"

"You betcha, Jeevesy. Have a listen." I nodded at the kitty carrier.

"Unhand me, you brute!" Ms. J wailed. "You filthy, treacherous hooman!"

I winked at the carrier. Her performance was a bit over the top, but not bad.

"Impressive," Mr. Jingles crackled through the intercom. "Please hold, sir."

After another long pause, Mr. Jingles' voice returned: "Mr. Fuzzy Pants will see you now. You may enter." A buzzer went off by the intercom and the gates swung open.

"Thanks, Jeevesy," I said. "You're a real pal. Just one more thing: Can I have two cheeseburgers, a large order of fries, and a strawberry shake? A fella gets hungry sitting at a drive-thru." I pulled the Studebaker forward into the drive without waiting for a response. Ms. J and I chuckled to ourselves.

I parked in the drive where it looped around in front of the mansion doors. Mr. Jingles stood stiffly at the top of the stairs. His fluffy cream-colored fur was immaculately groomed. Not a thread of his tuxedo was out of place.

I killed the engine, grabbed Ms. J's carrying box and the plastic bag full of nip, and got out of the car. Mr. Jingles trotted down the steps to greet me. He eyed the nip bag and the carrying box, then raised his chin as smug as you like. "Well done, sir," he said in his trained cat-butler singsong. "Mr. Fuzzy Pants will be quite pleased indeed."

"Well, you know I live to serve and aim to please, Jeevesy."

"Yes, of course, sir," Mr. Jingles said. He was trying to hide it, but I knew I was getting under his fur. His little mouth puckered into a sour, snobbish expression. "Very well, then. Right this way." He turned and led me up a winding cobblestone path to Mr. Fuzzy Pants' greenhouse. It seemed that the old cat had taken to sitting there quietly in the morning hours.

I followed Mr. Jingles inside the damp, sweltering pseudo-jungle. I'm no botanist, but I have to admit I was impressed by the sheer size of the greenhouse and its vast array of plant life. It bristled with tropical plants, orchids, ferns, palms, and some tall broad-leafed trees that created a canopy that cast a deep penumbra over the ground.

And lounging in that penumbra, cool as a cucumber, sat Mr. Fuzzy Pants. He was reclining on a cushion in one of those old-fashioned, high-backed wheelchairs. The kind with the little holes in their wicker backs. I always get this crazy impulse to stick my finger in those holes.

Mr. Fuzzy Pants was flanked on either side by his two henchmen, a couple of orange tomcat thugs who went by Mimsy and Muncy. Mr. Fuzzy Pants scoped the kitty carrier and the nip bag and grinned. His toadies scowled.

"I understand you have something for me," Mr. Fuzzy Pants said to me, still grinning.

I cocked my head. Raised an eyebrow: "I do."

I walked toward Mr. Fuzzy pants and stopped a few feet in front of his wheelchair. I set down the cat carrier and the bag of nip. Mimsy and Muncy tensed. The big boss cat waved them off with a dismissive swipe of his paw. He took a long look at the goods and clapped his paws together gleefully. "Well done, my boy! Well done! They said you were the best shamus in town and they didn't lie. Help yourself to some champagne and brandy if you like. You can has. I would have Jingles pour it for you, but alas, no thumbs." He held up a paw and mimed a pinching gesture.

"Don't mind if I do." I walked to the mini bar, feeling the greenhouse sprinklers spray a fine mist against my face. It was refreshing in the sweltering heat of the greenhouse. I poured a half glass of brandy from a crystal decanter, popped a bottle of champagne, and poured some bubbly on top of the brandy. I took a healthy swig. "That's the stuff," I said. I took off my Fedora and wiped my brow with the back of my hand. Put the hat back on. With the usual sideways, jaunty tilt, of course.

"Indeed, my boy," Mr. Fuzzy Pants smiled. "Well, now that you're refreshed, let's get down to business, shall we? You've done a fine job, lad. Quite fine. I think I'll give you an extra ten percent above your usual rate."

"That's very generous of you." I tipped the brim of my Fedora.

"Jingles, give the hooman the envelope," Mr. Fuzzy Pants commanded.

"Of course, sir," Mr. Jingles chimed. The catservant pulled a fat envelope from the inside of his tuxedo jacket with his teeth, then trotted over and handed me the envelope.

"Thanks, Jeevesy." I shoved the envelope into my trench coat pocket.

"Now if there's nothing further," said Mr. Fuzzy Pants, "I have some nip to organize, and…" He glared at Ms. J's carrier "someone has been a very naughty kitty."

"She has," I agreed. I sauntered over to the cat carrier and stood beside it. "There's just one thing."

"Oh?" Mr. Fuzzy pants said. "And what pray tell might tha—"

I reached down and unlatched Ms. J's kitty carrier. I drew a water pistol from my trench coat pocket. "Everybody freeze! Paws up!"

“But how can we do that?” Muncy asked. He wasn’t trying to be a smart guy. He just really was that dumb. “If we try to put all four paws up—“

“Shaddup, Muncy”! I snapped. I pointed the water pistol at him. “Everybody just get on your hind legs and—Nevermind! Just hold still, dammit!” I grunted in exasperation.

Mimsy and Muncy tensed again. They looked a bit froggy. Then they froze dead still. A red laser beam appeared right between Mimsy’s eyes. I glanced at my feet and saw Ms. J. She was gripping a laser pointer in her teeth. Her upper lip snarled. She pounced from her carrier, tackled Mr. Jingles, and sat on his back. The catservant struggled and squirmed, but it was no use.

“Release me at once!” Mr. Jingles wailed.

“No,” said Ms. J. She settled in and steadied the laser beam between Mimsy’s Eyes. At this point, the laser light became too much for Muncy to resist. He pounced full-force at the glowing red dot. Which, as I just said, happened to be trained on Mimsy's face. The two henchcats fell in a flailing tangle. And now they were both wildly chasing the red laser beam. Ms. J cackled gleefully and flashed the light beam all over the greenhouse. Mimsy and Muncy ran and leapt and crashed and careened everywhere the light led them.

Mr. Fuzzy Pants shook his head at the ineptitude of his lackeys. "My dear hooman," he said. "There must be some misunderstanding. I'm sure we can work something out."

I kept quiet.

"If it's a matter of money—"

I leveled my water pistol at the old boss cat.

"I don't understand, my dear fellow," he said. "What's all this about?"

"You're crooked, Fuzzy Pants, crooked. Your whole operation is crooked. Your cathouses. Your numbers games. Your cronies. Your poisoned catnip. How many lives have you destroyed? How many rugs?"

"Rugs? I don't under—"

"Hairballs, damn it! They ruin rugs! Well I say I've had enough! You're finished, Fuzzy Pants! Finished!"

"But my dear boy—"

"Shaddup, ya two-bit mug!" I motioned toward the door with my water pistol. "Everybody on your paws. We're all going to take a little ride. And no funny stuff, or I'll fill ya bums full of water, capishe?"

I picked up the nip bag and Ms. J's carrying case with my free hand and we shepherded the crooked cats to the Studebaker. I popped the trunk, pulled out four kitty carrying cases, then slammed the trunk shut.

"Everybody into a box," I ordered "You'll all have to share the back seat. Ms. J has shotgun."

The four crooked cats looked up at me with matching wide "oh shit" eyes.

***

So that's the story of how I got a cat. Don't worry about Mr. Fuzzy Pants, Mr. Jingles, Mimsy, and Muncy. I found them a nice home with four small children, where they can play all day long. From what I hear, they get to play cowboys and Indians and have tea parties and play dress-up all the time. And apparently they're downright docile now that they've all been neutered. Although Mr. Fuzzy Pants still likes to boss his lackeys around.

And don't worry about the rug. It took an extra cleaning, but I finally managed to get the stain up with some white wine and TSP.

As for me and Ms J., we're doing just fine. She's a good partner when I'm beating the streets, and a great partner when I'm on a stakeout. But on most nights, we like to stay in with some whiskey and a good old-fashioned *noir* picture. *Casablanca* is still her favorite.

THE ENORMOUS SPIDER

Erin Camille Jackson

He now felt certain that the cockroaches were in cahoots with the enormous spider hiding in his showerhead. A line had been crossed. The enemy had formed an alliance, an axis of evil, as it were. He could practically hear the little insect generals plotting their strategy. It was time for Jim to adjust his tactics.

When he woke up that morning he had that, today-is-the-day-I-get-you, kind of feeling as he loaded his handgun and sipped his herbal tea. Up 'til then he had enlisted all the usual plans of attack. He'd sprayed poison in every corner of his apartment, causing his eyes to swell shut and his nose to run. He'd planted sticky traps, which he, on occasion, discovered clinging to his pant leg. Of this he suspected the cockroaches as saboteurs. Though, clearly, the enormous spider was the brains of the operation. Jim had long ago resigned himself to showering at the gym. He'd tired of the spider judging and mocking his nakedness.

In some of his final desperate attempts to eliminate the invaders he'd visited the local herbal spiritualist shop, where he'd purchased demon-deterring candles. They made him sneeze. He'd burned sage until the smoke alarm asserted its protest. He'd even visualized his apartment as vermin-free, only to open his eyes to the sight of a curious cockroach audience attending the show, munching his leftovers as refreshments. Jim could swear that one even held a tiny ticket stub covered in web. That was the last straw. Jim dumped all his hippie weapons in the trash and bought a gun.

When he first entered Shamus's We Kill'em Pistol and Pawn he inspected a robust single barrel shotgun. Upon hoisting the enormous phallic beast to his shoulder he stumbled backward under the weight into a case of neglected wedding rings and silver belt buckles. The clerk tried to smother a self-righteous chuckle.

"Just like the spider," Jim thought with renewed rage.

No way was he going to give that eight legged pompous pest another excuse to taunt him. No, a smaller, lighter weapon would be better suited for the task anyway. After comparing the virtues of several different handguns he decided on a black slide-action nine millimeter side arm that made him feel like a special ops guy.

When Jim strode back into his apartment he had a swagger to his walk and could actually feel his muscles getting bigger from the pressure of the gun on his belt. He was a man now. He couldn't remember what he had been before he owned a gun, but clearly it was something other than *Man*. He grunted and adjusted himself before carefully placing the gun on his bedside table, right beside his embossed diary and his mentholated facial tissues. A single fat cockroach peered out from behind the tissues, wiggling his shiny antennae with interest. In a blink he turned and scurried off out of sight.

"Fine. Go warn them! It won't do you any good!" Jim called after the scout. However, as an afterthought, he rushed to slam the bathroom door, shoving a towel under to block the gap.

Jim decided that he'd done enough for one day. Just knowing his gun was there, ready, when the final battle began was a huge relief. He swaggered into the kitchen to prepare himself a pleasant dinner.

In the refrigerator Jim located a bundle of organic white asparagus, a jar of rosemary-infused olive oil cream sauce, a bright pink Alaskan salmon fillet wrapped in pristine butcher paper and tied with twine, and his favorite lightly pear-perfumed white wine. He was just about to begin cooking when he caught a glimpse of himself in the hallway mirror. In his crisply pressed white apron, delicate vegetables in hand, he felt a pang at the sight. This was not the image of a man who had just purchased a gun, a man who would shortly be going into combat against an army of roaches commanded by a wily spider possessed of super cunning.

Jim cast off his apron, returned the ingredients to their proper places in the well-organized refrigerator, and reemerged with a thick slab of steak and a domestic beer that one of his coworkers had left behind after his most recent brunch party. Yes, men eat steak. Men chug beer. And men shoot things!

A small battalion of roaches chirped amongst themselves from behind the coffee maker. They twitched their antennae agitatedly before one, in a clear show of defiance, grabbed up a crumb from the counter top and scuttled off. The others followed, chirping as they went.

"Yeah. You're scared now, aren't you? You can see that I am *Man*, and you are *Bug*." Jim felt very pleased with himself. Instilling fear in one's enemies is an important aspect of war. He thought he'd read that in *The Art of War* once.

That evening passed quite enjoyably for Jim. He ate his steak bloody. He drank his beer from the can rather than a frosted glass. All the while he was conscious of the nervous cockroaches watching him from their infinite hiding places. He watched some uber macho film on TV, paying extra attention to the gun fights. Afterward he washed his dishes and began to wipe down the counter, but paused when a beady pair of eyes met his.

A lone cockroach had bravely ventured out in search of what Jim felt would surely be his last meal. The small bug had nearly reached his objective, a tasty crumb at least the size of his head. The cockroach waited stone still. Jim unconsciously gave a slight smile. He turned away and placed the sponge on the sink. Then Jim headed off to bed.

Just before turning out the light Jim decided to check the bathroom door one last time. All was well. It was still closed and the towel was safely lodged under it. The evil spider was securely imprisoned in his tile and linoleum jail cell. It would be safe to sleep.

All night Jim dreamed of epic battles. Mighty titans fell to his ferocious blows. Legions of barbarians fled from his battle cry. And despots with eight legs begged for mercy from his execution squad.

In the morning Jim awoke confident and refreshed. He patted the gun on the table and yawned. Perhaps just the threat of firepower would be enough to dissuade the cockroach army. It was at that moment that Jim noticed something very unsettling. The towel he'd placed under the door was laying uselessly in the middle of the room. His eyes darted to the bathroom door.

"Dear God!" They've freed their leader!" It appeared that the cockroaches, in a supreme feat of determination and collaboration, had managed to push open the door.

Jim climbed out of bed. He tiptoed into the bathroom and, shaking, flung back the shower curtain. There, dangling jauntily from the showerhead, was the spider, swinging and possibly even humming to itself as it went.

"Yeep! Ahhh!" Jim squealed as he leapt two feet in the air, grabbing the gun and ammo as he fled for the kitchen.

In the kitchen Jim rummaged desperately through his pantry in search of his anxiety-reducing herbal tea. He needed something to settle his nerves. This was it. The time had come. He had made a show of force and the spider had called his bluff. He sipped gingerly at his herbal tea and carefully loaded his gun.

Just as Jim finished the last sip the troops appeared. From behind the coffee pot they marched in battle formation. To his left, from under the toaster, they were flanking. Jim set his jaw and furrowed his brow, snarling. He could hear their ranks closing in from the living room, their tiny feet clicking on the hardwood floor. He hoped they wouldn't leave scuff marks.

In a monumental act of defiance, Jim cocked his gun and aimed at the squadron of rotund cockroach infantry. His hands no longer shook. *Man* had gun.

BANG! Jim's shoulder jerked back with the force of the discharge. His ears rang. When he opened his eyes he saw a gaping hole in his travertine countertop and the remaining members of the squadron beating their way toward the hallway in retreat. Jim was momentarily distracted by the fact that two of the cockroaches seemed to be dragging their wounded comrades with them.

Jim regained focus, letting out a mighty, "Grwarr!"

Running into the hallway in pursuit he fired again. BANG! He'd taken out one team of roaches, along with his antique gilded mirror, which crashed musically around his feet.

Now, the reinforcements arrived. Jim shot into the living room. His sofa exploded in a puff of ethically-harvested down feathers and cartwheeling cockroach carcasses. The carnage was superb!

Another group of rascally roaches rushed past him toward the bedroom, nearly knocking him off his feet. They had captured his first edition Kafka.

"Terrorist Tactics!" Jim screamed as, BANG, he blew a hole through the floor, missing all but four of the minions.

Jim stumbled into the bedroom, blind with the intensity of battle. Some of the cockroaches held their ground, perched on his headboard, their antennae twitching menacingly.

BANG! The headboard splintered and smoked. The survivors rushed, en masse, through the open bathroom door.

With a courage Jim had never before known he rushed in after them. He was surrounded.

The enormous spider swung, smirking, from the shower head. And, all around Jim, the cockroach army was gathered. A trap!

BANG! Jim's toilet became a geyser raining down porcelain shrapnel all around. One chunk of the seat shot straight to the ceiling and cracked the light fixture.

Now or never. Jim steadied his aim at the evil spider who now hung perfectly still, glaring Jim right in the eye.

BANG! The shot whizzed past the spider, causing it to spin on its thread. Shower tiles gave way in a crumbling avalanche.

But, Jim saw none of this. The light fixture had dislodged and fallen from the ceiling. It bashed Jim directly on the top of his head, knocking him unconscious.

For a few moments all was silent. The cockroaches looked from one to another, antennae wagging wildly. Then the hush was broken. Three of Jim's neighbors, very disturbed by the ruckus, but unwilling to venture out until the battle sounds had faded, picked their way through the wreckage and into the bathroom. Hearing their approach, the roach troops retreated into the walls.

When the concerned citizens entered the bathroom they beheld their quiet, good natured neighbor unconscious, drenched in toilet water, amid the ruin of tile, blood matting his hair, and an enormous self-satisfied looking spider perched on his nose.

After a brief hospital stay Jim sold his apartment to a lovely couple, the Wilsons. Mr. Wilson recently acquired a gun permit and has been showering at the office.

The Lanai

Aaron A. A. Smith

The bell dinged, the up arrow blinked, and the elevator doors opened. The handsome yet unextraordinary man stepped into the posh yet unextraordinary lift.

He was immediately engulfed in a miasma of sickeningly cloying perfume. The cheap kind that reeked of synthetic flowers, decaying fruit, acrid vinegar, and whoredom. That was the routine, though. Some days the elevator reeked of cheap perfume. Some days it reeked of dog piss. Some days it reeked of both. Yes, some days were just special. Though still unextraordinary.

His head swam under the chemical warfare attack cloud of cheap whore perfume.

At least there were no other passengers in the elevator. Being sealed in that tiny space capsule, pressed in by yammering suburbanite strangers/neighbors made him anxious and aggravated. He couldn't breathe, let alone relax. Whenever he spied another passenger waiting for the lift, he would find an excuse to delay his approach. He would open the trunk to his car and pretend to root around. Or he would open the car door, pretend to search the seats and the floormats, then assiduously check the locks. Whatever it took to eat up a few moments until the elevator dinged and spirited away the other passenger. Then he could enter the lift alone. And breathe. Of course, sometimes, despite his best efforts, it was impossible to avoid the suffocating, awkward experience of riding the elevator with other people. Sometimes the doors peeled open, and there would be a person, or a group of people waiting. Pressing in on him. Chattering a dizzying and banal droning in his ears. Breathing.

But today, no such horrors awaited him. Just an empty elevator. He stepped in and swiped his fob in front of a sensor on the wall. A small light blinked red. He punched the button for his floor as the doors eased shut.

A low-quality 8 ½ by 11 computer paper printout had been plastered on the elevator wall. In big, off-kilter letters—the kind usually reserved for children's birthday party invitations—the flyer informed him, nay all who rode the shiny elevator with its glossy faux wood walls, that the building's social committee (what the hell kind of a building has such an abomination?) would be throwing a rooftop party on Sunday. In a smaller, less batshit crazy font, the flyer stated that the express purpose of this socially awkward soiree' was to greet any and all new residents of the building. All residents, however, were invited. Mexican appetizers would be provided. *Oh, goodie!* BYOB. *No free alcohol? And they admit that up front?* To top it all off, in what could only be interpreted as a badly misguided attempt to lure residents to the socially awkward gathering, the flyer was emblazoned with a pixelated photo of a group of old people chatting, or otherwise awkwardly socializing. He thought of a line that Raylan Givens had once delivered on *Justified: "I think I'd rather put my dick in a blender."*

The man glanced around the elevator and spotted another notice on the wall. A smaller sheet of paper, printed in a normal font, rested in a clear plastic tray that had been screwed into the side of the wall just above the awkward party flyer. Very professional, as far as elevator flyers went. The notice read:

It has come to our attention that the balcony doors in some of the units may become stuck when shut. Owners are responsible for the maintenance of the balcony doors. For maintenance and repair, we recommend… Blah, blah, blah, etc.

He didn't care to read the rest of the note.

The elevator reached his floor. The bell dinged, the arrow lit up, and the doors slid open.

***

The day started like any other. The man woke up sometime in the afternoon. Sickly yellow beams of light invaded his room through the edges of his pulled down blinds. His head felt heavy and foggy. A sharp pain shot from behind his right eye all the way to the top of his skull.

He had been up all night again. True, he had always had trouble sleeping. But his historical inability to sleep wasn't the problem. The problem was that wasn't *allowed* to sleep. Little distinctions can make all the difference.

The cacophonous sounds of the street below blared through the thick glass balcony doors and the drawn blinds of the man's bedroom. The sounds of the trolley: a computer-like, sterile muzak *ding dong*. The flat, choked-duck claxon of the horn. The garbled, unintelligible robot voice of the trolley driver emanating from a distorted speaker like the voice of a fast food drive-thru window operator. The sound of dozens of shuffling feet and the undulating locust hum of pedestrians and trolley passengers rang in the man's ears. The jerky, quasi-rhythmic shouts and ravings of a hobo served to complete the strange orchestra. *Another day in paradise.*

The man grunted long and low in his dry throat. He threw back the covers, rolled out of bed, put on the OR scrubs that served as his house robe, dodged the imposing mountain of floor clutter at his feet, opened the bedroom door, and hobbled blearily into the living room. There he was greeted by more of the sickly yellow afternoon light flooding through the half-drawn living room blinds. More yellow as he entered the living room/kitchen area of his apartment. Yellow sunflowers in a vase and a yellow balloon in the shape of a smiling sun on the kitchen island. A photograph of a yellow flower on the far wall of the living room.

It was a yellow day. The man felt yellow. Just like the sickly afternoon light.

He grabbed the big plastic jug of Canadian Club Whiskey from the kitchen island and poured a few fingers into his Jim Beam glass—he was no stickler for matching the brands of his liquor and glassware—and took a slow, deep sip. He snatched the TV remote from the coffee table and flipped on the old tube. *I guess it isn't really the tube anymore. All digital now.*

The familiar *Sportscenter* studio popped up on the screen. The anchors were talking about LeBron again. He tuned out the anchors' background panegyrics and focused his attention on reading last night's MLB scores as they scrolled on the ticker tape at the bottom of the TV screen. All of the big market teams had defeated all of the small market teams. His team, of course, was a small market team. Today was a travel day for them, so there was no game to look forward to tonight. *A sickly yellow day indeed.*

The man swigged down the remaining whiskey in his glass, put on a pot of generic brand coffee (selected purely as a low-cost kick of caffeine, as opposed to a gourmand experience), and poured himself a screwdriver while the coffee pot percolated.

He felt like throwing a couple of wrinkles into today's routine. It seemed only fitting. He turned off the TV and crossed the living room to his old record player. He sifted almost aimlessly through the record stacks until his fingers hit upon an old 45 single and stopped. "Sukiyaki" by Kyu

Sakamoto. As a child, he'd had a music box that played the tune. He wondered what ever had happened to it.

Kyu Sakamoto. He died in a plane crash in 1985. Same as Ricky Nelson. Bad year for flying crooners.

The man stood motionless, holding the old 45 single in his hands like a robot that had shut down in the middle of a task. He spooled for a moment, then rebooted, took the record from the sleeve, and slipped it onto the record player. He turned on the record player and lowered its arm. The needle slid into the circular grooves of the record. There was a comforting, lo-fi crackle, grainy and rough, yet smooth. The sound of time gone by. The sound of memory almost lost.

The song began to play.

The bittersweet tune and Sakamoto's dreamlike vocals demanded another whiskey. The man poured a couple more fingers of brown and sipped away, lost in the music. At the end of the song, he slammed the last swig in the glass and returned "Sukiyaki" to its place in the record collection. He then returned his attention to his screwdriver, taking a healthy slug as he walked into the kitchen.

The coffee was ready. He poured a draught of the harsh, acrid blend into a white coffee cup with a blue and green cartoon owl on the front. He Irished up the coffee, finished his screwdriver, then took a sip from the owl mug.

The man started to pull open the freezer to snatch a quick, microwaveable breakfast, then changed his mind. Today he felt like omelette rice. He had seen it once on a Japanese TV show and had wanted to try it ever since. But first he needed some music.

He walked back to his record collection and flipped through the stacks. His fingers instantly found what he was looking for: Mozart's Mass Requiem. It had been one of his favorite compositions ever since he had gone to see *Amadeus* at the movie theatre when he was seven-years-old.

He put the record on the turntable and slipped the needle into the groove. Again, that smooth, grainy crackle as the first notes rose into the air. Soft like a whisper, but dark and powerful underneath, hinting at the thunderous eruption of malevolent beauty and fury to follow. He closed his eyes and let the music flow through his senses like a part of his very being. The notes coursed through his ears, his head, his chest, and down the back of his neck.

Now he was ready.

He grabbed a knife and a cutting board from the dishwasher. Fetched some ham, onions, and mushrooms from the fridge to dice. Nuked a bag of instant rice. Cracked three eggs and whipped them up in a black ceramic bowl. He then pulled two cooking pans from the cupboard, slathered them with butter, and placed each pan on a burner on the stovetop. He poured the eggs into one pan, the ham, rice, and vegetables into the other. He swirled the pan of eggs in a languid, rhythmic circle, and stirred the ham, rice, and veggies with a big wooden spoon. When he deemed the time appropriate (not a moment before or after), the man dumped the rice, ham, and veggies on top of the circular sheet of cooking eggs, then folded the omelette into a pouch. He gave it about half a minute, then took out a spatula and flipped the omelette onto a plate.

Then he sat at the kitchen island, ate his rice omelet, drank his Irish coffee, and listened to Mozart.

When the man was done with breakfast, he decided to take a quick shower. He walked to the bathroom, turned on the lights, and glared at the face in the mirror. His beard stubble was looking a bit heavy today. He contemplated the act of shaving, but the thought alone made him feel exhausted. *Besides, it grows so damn fast anyway. Even when you're dead. Well, it doesn't actually* grow, *but as the corpse loses fluids and begins to desiccate, the skin shrinks, making it appear that the hair, beard, and fingernails have grown. Therefore Uncle Vania is a vampire and must be pinned to his grave with a wooden stake through his heart.*

The man turned the shower knobs and climbed under the cooling nozzle stream as the choir in the living room chanted *Rex Tremendae Majestatis.* There was something ominous and desperate about this section of the composition. *King of Awful*

Majesty. It reminded the man of the images of Hell in old Flemish paintings. Twisted. Tormented. Hopeless.

Salva me.

Salva me.

He soaped up, rinsed off, turned off the shower, toweled off, and stepped out of the shower. A single bead of water dripped down his back between his shoulder blades. He didn't bother to dry it. He walked back to the sink area, opened the medicine cabinet, and grabbed a jar of hair putty. He scooped out a dab of paste with his fingers and casually spread it through his hair. He leaned against the sink counter, took a long glance at himself in the mirror, and exhaled a deep, weary breath. He crossed the apartment to his bedroom and fished out a pair of boxers, a black t-shirt, and a worn pair of blue jeans from the dresser. He dressed and left the bedroom.

In the living room, the choir of Hell was gravely thundering their chant. *Confutatis! Maledictis!* He could hear their voices accusing, condemning, damning the desperate and beleaguered soul.

Flammis acribus addictis!

Darkness spread over the man's mind like a death shroud.

The choir of the condemned mournfully plead its response.

Voca me.

Voca me cum benedictis.

A prayer that can never be answered.

Gere curam mei finis.

The man poured himself another glass of whiskey. He stood and stared through the gap in the half-open living room blinds. He did not look downward at the street and the trolley tracks below. He looked straight ahead. At the empty office building that cast deep shadows and glared lifeless fluorescent light from the other side of the trolley tracks. At the red and blue neon OPEN sign pulsating beside the doors of the convenience store below, the letters reflected and flipped in the window across the way so that they looked like they had been written in a strange dialect that may have been an offshoot of Cyrillic. At a patchy-feathered pigeon limping back and forth on a ledge.

The man listened to Mozart's last composition as he watched the shadows grow outside and the yellow light retreat by inches.

And then he did something he had not done in a very long time. He put on his slippers and walked across his bedroom. He faced the drawn blinds that stood sentinel before the balcony and the outside world beyond.

He raised the blinds.

Lux aeterna.

The man squinted against the sudden flood of grimy yellow sunlight sinking steadily on the horizon. He braced himself. Then he opened the balcony door and stepped out onto the lanai. The balcony was small and cramped, and narrowed to a triangular point where the outer plexiglass safety rail and the inner gray-blue stucco wall converged.

The man stepped out onto the balcony. He shut the door behind him. A warm gust of early summer air lightly gusted into his face and rustled his hair.

He didn't approach the rail. Standing next to the rail made him feel like a part of the street and the people below. It made him feel like he was perched on a display shelf.

So he stood with his back nearly touching the door and looked to the horizon. The office building across the way. A few dubious markets and convenience stores. A series of unattractive modern apartment buildings rising into the sky like spines on the back of a monster. Scaffolding for the endless construction that accompanies each new wave of gentrification. The top of the dome of the public library, ever receding behind the ever emerging slew of new buildings. Soon the dome would disappear altogether.

The street below was oddly silent. Just a few straggling trolley commuters. It seemed as though the man had stumbled into that strange limbo between the afternoon rush of schoolchildren wrestling and shouting in Spanglish, the standard rush hour of commuters heading home from work, and the late-night matinee of hobos staggering and screaming prophetic doom alongside the occasional drug deal or trick being turned. It reminded the man of a Tom Waits song, only without any romance or beauty.

Without turning around, the man reached behind his back and pressed down on the door handle. It was locked. As he knew it would be.

The man could have flagged down somebody on the street below and had them call for help. He could have kicked down the patio door. But he was just too tired. So he did nothing.

The man closed his eyes and took a deep breath. The world went silent. When he opened his eyes, he saw the lanai as he had always dreamed it would be. High shoots of bamboo and potted palms screened out the outside world. Little bonsai trees lined a glass table in the center of the patio. A Japanese fountain trickled serenely in the corner.

He thought about all of the things he wanted to do: travel the world. Be there at the ballpark to see his team finally win a World Series. Watch an Olympic Games in person. Record an album. Write a novel…

But he was never going to do any of those things. Because he was trapped.

You think you're treading water, but there's really no such thing. You're just sinking bit by bit like a setting sun. If you're not swimming, you're sinking.

And that's exactly what the man did. He sank down until he was sitting with his back resting against the glass door of the lanai.

And for the first time in his life, he was free.

THE BURIAL OF JONAS SNAWLSKI

Erin Camille Jackson

Rarely has such a motley funeral procession been seen as the one set on burying Jonas Snawlski. Two hefty guys slowly lugged his body up the hill while a third, scrawny fellow followed behind with the digging implements, pausing every thirty paces to look 'round for ghosts.' Tails Only Tommy was tired of this job. If Patsie hadn't been so persuasive he'd have never even been on that damn hill, in the damn dark, with the damn rain, lugging that damn body around.

Across the street a little yellow shack of a house bore witness to the deed. From her seat at the window, Patsie watched the procession with about as much feeling as she'd had when the kettle boiled over on the stove. A shame, but done is done. Nobody quite knew how she'd done it. They wondered, naturally. But, knew that they would never, ever, ask her. Those sorts of questions tend to put an undue strain on friendships.

Snawlski had been the kind of man who accidentally cheated on his wife, while hiding out at his voluptuous second cousin's house, because he kind of forgot to pay his bookie. These kind of men very quickly become the kind of men most often described in past tense. It's no wonder that this kind of man was also the kind of man buried under the cover of dark by three thugs with stolen shovels. It just naturally follows.

When Patsie called Tails Only Tommy that night it was just starting to drizzle. The fire-flies were still dancing above the high un-mowed grass, and the heat of the day hadn't yet lifted. The last of the waning afternoon's crickets chirped a call and response to one another before retiring for the evening. Thick putty colored clouds covered over the bruised sky, further dimming the light.

Tommy piled the crew in the back of his robin's egg blue and red-dirt rust covered pick-up and headed to Patsie's house. He wasn't sure what the problem was, but he felt confident that if it involved fuckin' Snawlski he'd need the boys for backup. Snawlski tended to fight dirty. Once, he even bit Lanky Lewie just below the kneecap. That's just not gentlemanly. Tommy popped open the glove compartment, checking to make sure he'd brought his buck knife.

As they pulled up the gravel drive they could see Patsie silhouetted in the light of the electric bug zapper. She was wearing her long robe and smoking her Marlboro Red. She squinted a little in the glare of the truck's one working headlight.

"You ever gonna get that damn thing fixed? Been over a month since you hit that deer." She took a final drag off her cigarette, flicked it to the ground, and stubbed the butt out with her bare foot.

"I know. Just not gotten 'round to it yet. Where's Snawlski? He been breakin' shit again?" Tommy peered around, "Ya' know you can call Sheriff Dale if he gets too rough." By this time the whole crew; Tommy, Lanky Lewie, and Skunk were all standing in Patsie's dandelion-infested yard. Skunk had a tire iron in one enormous, grease-stained paw. He'd grabbed it from a workbench at The Garage when told where they were headed.

Patsie looked at the tire iron for a moment, then at deep crags in Skunk's stubbly face. "Not gonna need that this time, Skunk," and she gestured for them to follow her around back.

They wiped their work-booted feet on the plastic grass mat as they walked, single file, through the open front door. They passed through the living room/dining room, careful not to brush up against the dusty pink, overstuffed couch, adorned with a white crocheted doily. They all squeezed into the kitchen that Patsie had just re-wallpapered in a motif of marching ducks against a field of blue and white stripes. They each commented that it sure did look classy. Patsie held open the screen door and they followed her out.

"He's there." She gestured into the darkness just off the crooked concrete back steps.

Tails Only Tommy and the boys tried to see what she pointed at, but all they could make out was a big lump. A big lump, half leaning against the side of the house. A big lump that appeared to be wearing flannel and blood.

"My God. Is that him?" Lewie asked as soon as his eyes adjusted.

"Yeah."

"Patsie, you gotta tell me he's drunk, right?" Tails Only Tommy asked carefully.

"Uh-uh," she said as she shook her head.

"He's not actually…"

"Yeah. He is. I checked." Patsie wiped an invisible speck of dirt from her robe.

"Did *you*…" Skunk began, but was stopped short by a swift clop to the head, administered by Tails Only Tommy.

Tommy then responded to Miss Patsie the only way he felt a gentleman could when a lady was faced with an unpleasant situation. He said he would take care of it, and she needn't worry anymore. He had always had a weakness for her charms. She could get him to do anything. Once, she even got him to watch one of those foreign films with her 'cause Snawlski was off doing whatever it was he did. He told Lanky Lewie to go find some shovels and meet them back there. Luckily, the neighbors had left their shed unlocked, and Lewie nabbed two and a pickaxe. Patsie went back inside and plopped in a kitchen chair right by the window.

Across the street from Patsie's little house rested a lonely cemetery that had, over the years, fallen victim to neglect, either from the fact that the dearly departed who made it their residence were, in fact, not so dear to those whom they'd departed, or that all those they'd departed had now, themselves, departed as well. Either way, it had been years since a grounds person had plucked a weed or raked a plot. And the gate hung precariously from its rusted hinges. The streetlights had burned out, and no one had thought to replace them. Being across from a cemetery had had the benefit of greatly reducing the property value of the little yellow house, making it affordable on Patsie's beautician's salary.

The two larger thugs grabbed the body by each leg while Lewie followed, shovels in one hand and pickaxe poised to ward off the advances of unfriendly spirits. He wished there'd been someone else bringing up the rear. The undead were not the sort of opponents he wanted to encounter. Lewie had a healthy fear of all things supernatural and was struggling desperately to remember the prayers the Sunday school teacher had tried to teach him. Nothing of real substance came.

"Our Father who…who is so good…give me this day. I mean night…" He fumbled for the words. "Ah, hell, Jesus, please don't let them ghosts eat me and leave my gnawed on body for the coyotes to finish up!"

"What the hell you babbling on about? Are you having a fit? Cause I will come back there and bash your fuckin' skull in with that shovel if you don't shut up," Skunk muttered into the darkness without looking back. He meant it, too. Skunk was not a man of empty threats. It takes some brains for empty threats.

After a short time, the crew had crossed the pitted asphalt of the street and were approaching the gate of the cemetery. Apparently, there had been some difficulty when Tails Only Tommy failed to see a particularly large pothole in the road. He'd stumbled a bit, nearly dropping the leg that was his charge. This caused Skunk to trip, as he was too busy adjusting Lewie's attitude to notice flaws in the road ahead. The torso of the body plopped directly into the rut with a dissatisfied splash. And it seemed as though Jonas Snawlski would be forced to make this his new home.

"Hell. He's stuck," Tails Only Tommy grumbled.

He yanked at his leg while Skunk yanked at the other one. But the body refused to move. Lewie was horrified. His most basic instincts took over. He gripped hard one of the shovels. Raising it above his head, he walloped the dead body vigorously on the backside. Three times. Little was achieved by this exercise, except that Snawlski's shoe jarred loose and catapulted itself into the darkness. Lewie futilely watched for it to land before dropping his tool and reaching his ridiculously long arms into the muck to dislodge their burden.

Snawlski's shirt had snagged on a rock. After much cursing, they managed to free the body from the offending snag. By this time the rain was mounting a full-scale attack. The three live men and the one dead man were now soaked through.

Once in the cemetery they were faced with a new dilemma. The damn place was built on a hill. A hill that now had become a virtual mudslide over which they must traverse. Nothing to be done but drag his sorry ass up that hill. It was slow going for a while. And, once, Tommy and Skunk lost their grip. It wouldn't have been such a disaster if Lanky Lewie had had his eye on the ball. But, instead, he was shooting furtive glances behind him every few steps, on the watch for the undead.

"Shit, Lewie, look out!" Tommy cried as the body began to slide down the hill toward the unsuspecting man.

"What?" Just then, with a THUMP and a WUMP, Jonas Snawlski took out Lanky Lewie. The body knocked him off his oversized feet. Lewie dropped on top of it and the two of them tumbled, cartwheel style, in an avalanche of mud. They passed the crumbling stone monuments to Aunt Eunice; Wallace Henderson, beloved husband and father; and Grandma Clay, born? Died 1921. They came to a muddy, tangled halt about halfway down the hill.

"He's got me! He's got me! Help!" Lanky Lewie wailed out into the dark.

"He don't got you. Get up from there. Quit playin' around with the body…ain't respectful." Tommy pried the two loose and suppressed a chuckle.

Once again, the boys began the hike up the cemetery hill. This time, it was even more troublesome since Snawlski had stubbornly taken on a thick coating of mud. But, they managed to drop him on a nice flat space of land that, thankfully, was not currently occupied. None of them were in the mood for digging up some other dead body. One stiff was quite enough.

"Why don't we take a breather? Hey, Skunk, you got your flask on you?" Tommy perched his rotund form on top of a gravestone that seemed reasonably stable and wiped his forehead with the back of his hand.

"Nah, I forgot it in the truck. How 'bout you, Lewie?"

Lewie had lost his flask in a poker game the night before to Snawlski, himself, and was feeling a little bitter about the matter. He swore Snawlski had been cheating the whole game, but never could figure out how he'd been pulling it off. This wasn't the first time Lewie had been the victim of their now departed friend's tricks. When they were kids Snawlski had bet Lewie one big hopping toad against Lewie's prized lucky rabbit's foot that he could run home faster. When Lewie arrived, there was Snawlski, sitting on the front porch, just grinning. Apparently, Snawlski knew a short cut through the woods. When they were teens Snawlski repeatedly stole Lewie's girls and had been known for cheating at baseball. Lanky Lewie was most bitter about the flask, though. It had been a gift from his Pop.

"Well, check his damn pockets. Hell, he might just have it on him," was Tails Only Tommy's response. He was generally a very practical man.

"Son of a bitch!" Lewie retrieved a slightly muddied flask from Snawlski's breast pocket. "And it's full, too! Damn!"

The three thugs stood around the body of Jonas Snawlski, leaning on the tools they would soon use to bury him, and drank his booze out of the flask he'd cheated off of Lanky Lewie. The rain was slowing now and the moon made a halfhearted, partial appearance from behind a bulbous cloud, lending a faint shimmer of opalescent white to the graveyard, which made it easier to see where they needed to dig. None of the men spoke a word for several minutes 'til Tommy announced it was time to get back to work.

"But first I gotta take a piss." He wandered over to a tree just downhill from the boys and walked around behind it to face the road. "Y'all get started without me."

From where Tommy stood he could see all the way down the hill and to the little yellow house across the way. He wondered what Patsie must be doing right now. He imagined he could see her shadow move past the kitchen window and into the living room. She was probably making herself a drink. Patsie drank whiskey, like the rest of them.

In his mind he pictured the scene.

Patsie carried her drink back to the chair by the window. She stared out into the night, but she couldn't make out the players anymore. She kept watching anyway. She would stay like that until the job was done and Tommy knocked on her door to say goodnight. She would smoke one cigarette after another, down to the brown nub, when it singed her acrylic fingernails. The ashtray would be over-full, and the room would be hazy with smoke. She wouldn't bother to open a window. Why should she? The ice in her drink would make tinkling noises like wind chimes when she swirled it. She'd like that sound and would swirl it over and over, just to hear it. She'd think about turning on the radio, for just a moment, and then fix another drink instead. The sound of the carpet swishing under her now slippered feet as she passed back to the kitchen would annoy her because it would seem louder than usual, and louder than the music of her ice cubes. She would frown, but just until her feet touched down on the linoleum, when the ice cube melody and the soft whisper of exhaled smoke would be the only sounds in the empty house. She would stare into the night again.

Skunk and Lanky Lewie made good time digging the grave. The ground was soft and they were accustomed to hard work. Tommy picked up a tool and diligently hoisted ground into the air. It landed in a pile with a heavy and hollow drum smack. The rhythm of their work made a kind of regular beat in the empty graveyard. They kept time with the shovel loads and the occasional grunt. Soon they had a hole large enough for a grown man. Lewie stood in the bottom of the pit and estimated that it must be over four feet deep. They all three agreed that a slightly shallow grave would be good enough under these circumstances. Skunk and Tommy dragged Lewie up out of the hole by his arms. They peered down at their handiwork.

"We should try to hurry this up. Ought to get out of here while it's still dark." Tommy broke the silence.

"Yep," replied Skunk.

"Yep," replied Lewie.

Tails Only Tommy and Skunk resumed their positions, grasping the feet, while Lanky Lewie lifted Snawlski under the armpits. They carried him over to the hungry hole of a grave they'd dug and made ready to toss him in. The body hung from their powerful grip over the precipice.

"On three," Tommy ordered.

"One…Two…Three."

With a great heave, the limp body of Jonas Snawlski fell four feet into the filthy earth. It landed neatly to rest at the bottom of the hole his friends had dug, with stolen tools, in the middle of the night, in the sloppy rain. It lay there, still and soundless. It lay there with its face skyward, eyes closed against the water that dripped off strands of disheveled and matted hair. It lay there, oblivious to the shovels full of red clay that were dumped over it. It lay there unknowing, dead.

Tails Only Tommy threw the first shovelful down, then Skunk, then Lanky Lewie. It was faster work than digging had been. They were anxious to finish up this chore and get home. They all had work in the morning. And they would get precious little sleep as it was. Bit by bit the grave filled up. Tommy tossed the last chunks of earth onto the plot and patted it down. It was done.

"Any of that whiskey left?" He asked as he dropped his shovel.

"Yeah. Ya' want some?" Lanky Lewie handed the flask to his friend. They stood around the grave, once more passing booze between men tired from a long night's work.

Tommy stared off again at the little yellow house. Just then the moon fought its way from behind the cloud and illuminated the three men in a blanket of whiteness. He knew she could see them now. She could see that it was finished. He saw her shadow move away from the kitchen window, like a ghost floating on the night air. He knew she would make one last drink. She would empty the ashtray and turn out all the lights in the house except the porch light. She'd wait on the living room sofa until Tommy knocked on the door. He knew all that.

"He was a bad man." Skunk spoke as if to himself.

"He was." Tommy said simply.

Tommy imagined what his friends might have been thinking while standing by that newly-made grave in the moonlight.

They might have thought of long, humid nights on Snawlski's front porch, swapping hunting stories. Or, they might have remembered when the four of them rescued a stray, mangy mutt and took turns feeding it 'til it became the best guard dog The Garage ever had. Or, they might have recalled a fishing trip, a lifetime ago, when four boys thought summer would never end and nothing could ever change.

At least that's what Tommy had been thinking about.

Lanky Lewie just gave a brief nod and picked up the tools. The three of them walked down the hill and across the street to the little yellow house. The others waited in the truck while Tommy stepped up on the porch.

She answered his knock by opening the door just a crack. Tommy wiped his forehead with his hand.

"Goodnight, Miss Patsie."

"Goodnight, Tommy."

WAR

Erin Camille Jackson

He'd removed the mirrors from the walls. The bathroom mirror was the hardest. It had been bolted in. Now, there was a gap, a space that led between his bathroom to his neighbors'. The little tin backing to their medicine cabinet was his face-level friend. He could hear their every morning move. Every toothpaste-filled conversation and every pointless argument. It was a thin metal window opera, revealing his fellow lodgers' world.

Without the mirrors he could be someone else. No battle scars or distorted, yet over examined, memories. He could just exist. However, that was its own pain. To be, and to be with it all, caught up inside…It could go a few ways. The darkness of non-reflection was taunting him. It told his secrets in a way that only blankness could. What if it had been otherwise?

He shook his head. It hadn't been otherwise. The guns had fired, over and over again. The bombs had dropped on tiny villages of sand and palm, turning them into firebirds, expanding their wings above the semi-mountainous hills and umbrella-tufted trees. The screams reverberated in his head like a perverse song. The sound was stuck, rotting in there, on perpetual repeat. The soundtrack that taunted his faculties was supported by a mind movie of the melting, waxen faces of peasants, blown land mines (theirs and ours) cracking and tearing men he'd known apart as they popped and bounced into bloody piles of jigsaw pieces, along the otherwise silent road of rusty powder dirt. It hadn't been otherwise…and he was always, every day, still there. The smell of those crispy palm trees melting in the distance putrefied in his nose.

He shuffled out of the bathroom and into the tiny kitchen of his studio apartment. He didn't entertain, so the functional nature of the flat suited him. The thought of random hordes of damnable people tromping into his abode was really enough to drive him back into the sanctuary of his bed. All he needed was there, and the superfluous did not have any place. The ordered nature gave him some minor comfort.

Coffee on and gurgling…

He let his glance travel over the kitchen island, into the living room, and rest on the black and silver keys of his Smith Corona typewriter. It was waiting. He knew it watched him. In a few minutes he would be compelled to sit with it and hammer out yet another letter to another grieving family member. The typewriter didn't even seem to mind the sadness. It just banged away like indoor machine gun fire.

He sipped his coffee and prepared for battle. He seated himself, stiffly erect, in the now cracked wood and cane chair. The old fashioned kind, with tiny holes systematically marching across the back that made him unconsciously push his finger into them every time he came near it. It was part habit and part comfort ritual. The tiny red impression of a circle on the pad of his index finger was so regular, and simple, and predictable.

Facing the typewriter and readying its thick stock paper, locking it in place for the frightening rollercoaster ride of writing, he remembered. He stared at the paper, waiting for the memory portion of the ride to fully crank into clacking motion. The memory was clear, always.

Walls, as the other men had nicknamed him, had always written little stories and poems. This continued while he was doing his tour in the Army. The dabblings surprised him with their darkness and their nostalgia. They were like imaginary sepia photos of the disquieted ramblings in his brain.

Late at night the other men began requesting readings. They liked the somber nature of his stories. They, somehow, seemed to calm a group of men who had every right to be frightened, who were frightened. It became a ritual among the soldiers who were all facing the unfathomable and unbearable realities in the morning. Some would, of course, not make it back for the next night's reading, the audience being depleted by war.

One afternoon, Walls clearly recalled, a fellow solider approached him after chow. It had been an unusually calm day. But, the day before, they'd lost Don Mayfield, Freddie, and Little Butch. They had been devoted members of the literary circle. The solider who approached Walls was named Sam. Sam's face wore a perpetual shadow. It took him a few bumbling attempts to find, then organize, his thoughts into words. When he finally got sorted, he requested that if, or when, any of the members of their fraternity of soldiers died Walls would write to their families.

"The Army does that." Walls replied, cautiously.

"No. Not like it should. They send some form letter. Same for every dead man…says nothing. It tells nothing." Sam averted his eyes as he confided in Walls.

"Why do you think I'll do any better?"

"The stories. Your stories. It's important that our people are told who we were, here, before we died."

Walls felt cold. It wasn't something you could really refuse. It was too big to do, but way too big to ignore. He reluctantly agreed, childishly hoping that maybe they'd all just survive, and he'd never be called to his task.

The next day their unit was almost entirely wiped out. Sam was among the casualties. Walls survived the war, at least in body. He would go home to his bed, his coffee maker, and his typewriter.

***

Walls had tried to write the letters when he first got back. But, his own trauma and grief wouldn't move the keys. Every clap, clap, clap drove up terror and the deafening soundtrack of the war. So he closed his eyes instead, rising from bed every morning, incapable of doing battle with the Smith Corona typewriter on his desk. He was incapable of facing down the memories.

This went on for a few years. It consumed him with guilt. He was shamed daily by his cowardice. Then came the shame at the shame. He no longer slept. The men's stories called out to be written, to be told. He had to respond.

A day came, just a regular day, when Walls found himself sitting at the desk. He was surprised to see he'd loaded the paper and had placed his hands at the keys. He'd not been aware of doing any of it. His heart contracted, squeezing the agony out of it through short, quick taps on the keys. It beat out the first words of the first letter, painfully. But they were true words.

***

The first letter Walls wrote was to Don Mayfield's mother. It opened up all the trauma he'd been trying to bury. It was a reburial and a resurrection through telling. Only he was telling Don Mayfield's story. He told about the unit banning Mayfield from singing cause he couldn't carry a tune. He told about his friend's ability to march harder and longer than any of the other men, and how that inspired them when they thought they'd drop where they were. And Walls told his dead buddy's mother about the terrible loss he felt. At the end he signed it, ceremoniously addressed and sealed the envelope, and finally sent it out of himself to its intended. Then Walls slept.

Since that first letter he had trudged through his list of the deceased men from his unit. Some days he couldn't bring himself to even approach the life and death recorder on his desk. His own disturbances and nightmare daydreams were too surface close. He'd retreat to his room, in hope of finding rest. But on those days it did not come. Walls did not sleep.

As time marched forward he was able to type more and more letters. Each one was a battle, but each left him a little healed. His wounds were gradually knitting as he recalled the wounds of his fellow men. It was still a long and arduous process, but he was progressing daily now.

Monday he wrote to Freddie's widow.

"Freddie's humor kept us cheered when we were most in need of laughter. He even drew comics about the unit's various antics."

Walls also told her that there had been a quieter and more reverent version of Freddie.

"He spoke to me, one night, of the unfathomable nature of, 'putting pieces of special people into body bags'. He simply shook his head after speaking this observation and returned to the task facing us all."

Walls wrote to another soldier's father about the man's faith. That man had refused to go to sleep without saying prayers for himself and the other men, whether or not they wanted them. Walls also told another side.

"James once told me he was convinced that death was following him, personally, but that death or God kept killing the wrong person."

Walls wrote about the horrors of friendly fire incidents; the cold, rain drenched nights; and men bonded together. He wrote of fear equally with valor. A promise had been made to tell these men's stories, not to concoct fantastic tales of fictional heroes. They were real heroes, and they had been flawed. He shared the flaws and greatnesses alike, in each of his letters.

The list got smaller. He had fewer nightmares. He realized, on a Friday, that there was only one letter left to write. The ordeal was nearly completed. All he had to do was to compose and convey this final portrait of a fellow soldier. But, he knew he'd been putting this one off. Day after day he'd moved this name to the bottom of the list. Now it was the list. One name. Sam.

Sam.

Sam had entrusted him with the lives and deaths of these men. Just as the Army had issued a rifle, Sam had issued paper and ink. It was Walls' final mission of their war. He was so close. Sam had died the day after commissioning Walls to write. He occasionally wondered if Sam had known somehow, or suspected, that his time had come. Not that it made much difference either way. The letter was waiting to be written. There were no more excuses.

He touched the holes in the back of the withered wooden chair. His finger bore the perfect red circle, a thing whole and finished, evidenced on his person. This was a comfort. Something complete. It felt like there should be gray rain pinging off his roof, but there wasn't a sound. The sky only held the weight of indulgent morning fog. He was grateful for the dimness, at least. Black and white words composed against the grayness of the air. He loaded the weighted, stiff paper into the waiting maw of the typewriter. He faced the menacing blank page.

In some cultures, when the dead have no family to mourn them, no one to miss them, or cling to their decaying memory, the mourning is assigned to a random person. It doesn't matter who this person is. That person is the mourner of a stranger. That ghost is their ghost.

Sam had no people.

He had no parents or siblings. He had no wife or sweetheart. He was young, and all of his friends had died in that war. No one to miss him. Walls blinked, blindly, at the typewriter. To whom do you address the letter of a person who left no one behind? Some amount of time passed. The light in the room shifted. The coffee had long ago gone cold. The paper was waiting for commands. Walls felt his fingers find the keys, as they had for all the other letters he'd composed. They started their tap, tap, tapping before he knew he was typing.

"Dear Walter Arthur Robbins (Walls),

Sam died in the war with others that you knew. He was younger than some, not as young as others. He loved stories, and might have written his own one day. He was hardened by the battles. He was afraid of the huge balls of flame that exploded and thrust themselves into the sky. They gave him violent nightmares, such that he said if he ever got home he'd never be able to sleep without a light on again. He didn't make it home. But, he tasked you with the lives and deaths of the men you both knew. He knew that a man is not one thing or one event. He knew that you had all changed and that the you that you had become needed to be told. He made sure these stories would be written, even though he had no one to read his. You will be Sam's mourner. His decaying memory is in your care…"

When Walls finished he signed the final letter, addressed it, and placed it in his pocket. The typewriter sat, emptied of paper. He sat, emptied of his task. He eventually stood up from his desk and reached around the typewriter for the case lid. It was heavy and a bit dusty. He closed the lid. He wiped the dust off of the monogramed plate affixed to the front. It was a simple rectangle. In the metal were carved the initials, W.A.R.

FAMINE

Erin Camille Jackson

"Take a memo, Maggie." Felix spoke into the Dictaphone. He usually started his statements with such an imperative toward his long loyal secretary, Maggie.

"Maggie, I'm hungry…not for food or…well, I have bourbon in here. But, I'm hungry for the next step. I think it's mealtime, and this account is my goddamn entrée."

Felix finished his tumbler of bourbon and paced back to his desk. The desk was overflowing with stock photos, vague illustrations, juvenile research folders, and cigarette ashes. He blew the top layer of ashes from the photo of a ridiculous blonde with too much hair and nothing resembling personality. Felix thought he recognized her. He did. She'd fucked some balding guy in the casting department and abandoned her cheap knockoff lace panties, as proof of her ambition, on the new copier machine. Felix chuckled into his glass. The absolute patheticness of human nature. It never ceased to amuse. They are all so hungry. They're famished for that something more, even just something else.

Of course, Felix had that affliction, too. He needed to rise from his current situation. He needed to dominate. This account was the fuel he required to perform at optimal level. He must land this account, and produce the most perfect ad ever to confront the meager minds and blinded drone souls of the drooling public plebeians. He must feed them just enough that they called out for more. They were starving for direction, starving for the lovely commodities, starving for the ability to proclaim, "I own this, just like everyone else of my kind."

Felix would graciously sell them their darling treasures, and fill their soulless bellies with his satiating wares. He shoved the litter off his desk to make room for his yellow legal pad and his bourbon glass. It was time to start cooking up some gourmet ideas for this ad campaign. No use feeding the masses the moldy concepts of his juniors. They consistently disappointed him with their lack of vision.

"Maggie, take a memo addressed to the morons working…slacking…under me." Felix refilled the frosted glass receptacle he favored for midmorning bourbon. It was a relic from the thirties, heavily weighted and comfortably rounded to fit in his large hand. It reminded him of a tulip bulb.

"Tell them that I am sick of rejecting their primary school attempts at art and metaphor. Their ideas are wilted. They provide no sustenance. They afflict me with pangs of hunger, even as I consume them. The very paper being wasted by these incompetent offerings nauseates and offends my senses. I have regurgitated them into the waste basket in hopes of cleansing my desperate palate of the putrid, vapid, and indigestible material they have submitted."

Felix stood silent for a moment, organizing the, as yet, thin ideas mixing around in his brain. He closed his eyes against the midmorning light streaming in from the floor to ceiling featureless window panes. The cool, anxious yellow of this light bothered him. It felt hostile, yet intimidated. Felix let out a harsh breath and returned to his Dictaphone composition.

"Maggie, let them know that I expect them to serve up three new ideas, with the artwork accompanying, by the start of the day tomorrow. The timer is ticking on this one. That is all for now."

He buzzed the ever diligent Maggie and she came to take the Dictaphone away for transcription. She didn't say a word. Her usual silence pleased Felix. She was his favorite office worker. No stomach cramp-inducing chatter from her. Once the solid beige door closed and he was left alone he slumped into the leather swivel chair behind his still disorderly desk.

He could hear the incessant conversation radiating from the adjacent hallway. The minions were, as usual, overindulging on takeout luncheon while ignoring the tasks at hand. Their shrill laughter and grotesque chuckles gave him enough indigestion that he rarely bothered with his own midday meal. He fed his hunger with the work. If he got the work just right it could feed him for days.

For some reason he felt a deep desire for this particular ad campaign. He needed it. He hungered for it more than any campaign he could remember. He was so close. The aroma of satisfaction taunted him every minute of the day. It felt too real and ripe. Felix started sketching out ideas in hasty shorthand sentences. It would come. He knew it would come.

The day rambled on with rejected ideas and neglected cigarettes. His brain acquired lubrication from the trusty bourbon as the light slowly fell and faded, retreating into the Neverland regions, until fully replaced by blackness that was only broken by fluorescent squares of office lights. Finally, Felix surrendered to his throbbing shoulders and cramped hand. The bourbon glass nestled itself to sleep on the bar cart. The desk chair slid into its alcove, keeping watch over the plethora of ideas from the day. Felix gathered his stiffly formed hat and London Fog raincoat before trudging out into the evening world, bound for home and bed, aware of his nagging desire to persist tomorrow.

***

"Take a memo, Maggie." Felix had arrived at the office a good deal earlier than usual. He'd slept at home, but in his suit. He'd fallen asleep working on the ad. It was getting closer. A fragile frame was building in his, admittedly, vertigo-afflicted head. It could almost encapsulate the idea. This was progress. But, he still felt a carnal need. It wasn't ready yet.

"Perhaps the morons could present their ideas together. I can ridicule and reject them all at the same damn time."

Felix poured a breakfast bourbon and hoped that Maggie might bring him a bagel from downstairs. He might have forgotten dinner during the work process last night. It was a mistake he often made. The light in his office began to change subtly, but enough to alert him that the place should be filling up with worker bees. Maggie would most certainly be in by now. As he thought this there was a reliably comforting knock on his door.

"Come in." He straightened his tie and sat up tall, like a school boy.

Maggie entered with the hoped for bagel in hand. She silently retrieved the Dictaphone and deposited the still warm breakfast on Felix's desk. He slowly consumed his bagel and his second breakfast bourbon while awaiting the anxious appearance of his underlings. He anticipated bland and tasteless ideas to come. Felix stared at the door as he gnawed at his bagel, getting crumbs on his desk and lap, wiping them off, onto the hideous avocado green carpet that was being consistently neglected by the vacuuming talents of housekeeping.

After a while, his staff knocked and then entered his office, without being acknowledged. They lacked manners. They had all been raised by crass parents who had more money than class, and seemed to value self-esteem above dignity and respect. They bothered Felix immensely. He detested their starved expressions. They were still gumming down baby food slop, where he wanted saline raw oysters, obscenely hearty bone marrow, and crisp white asparagus in a delicate white wine sauce. He might crave a nice steak on a Friday night out at the bar. But, he never desired a lobster dinner. Their crustacean eyes looked too deeply into his own. They knew something soulful. Felix was certain that those lobsters knew far more than his minions now standing before him.

"Well?" He lit a cigarette and checked the level of his bourbon. "Let's hear what you people have deemed acceptable for presentation." Felix inhaled deeply at his smoke and awaited disappointment.

Ben What's- His-Name volunteered to speak first.

"Well…It's a new and improved stereo sound system. The sound is big. It's smaller than its predecessor."

Felix crushed out his cigarette. "Glad to hear you read the damn material. Now what? Let's go."

Ben started again, after a quick glance at his coworkers. "Maybe it's something romantic. It's like, because it's small you can be in an intimate space with your girlfriend and still hear excellent music quality?" Ben swallowed hard and stepped back to the safety of the group.

Felix stood up and crossed to the bar cart in order to refill his dry glass. He heard the ice clinking. He inhaled the deeply sweet and burning aroma of his drink before speaking.

"It has two problems. First, and most blatantly obvious, it does not address the powerful sound that this new stereo system has. Second, and perhaps even more frustrating, is its surface romantics. Who are these people? It could be an ad for a blanket or a small television. There are the same two silly romantics in every popcorn, hot chocolate, and ice cream ad. No. No. Next!" Felix sat back in his swivel chair, turning it a bit in absent minded frustration.

"Ben, you are desperate and your ideas are desperate. You'll never feed that desperation with this greeting card romance. Go out. Get a drink…alone. See you in the morning. Didn't I say 'next'?"

Lance stepped forward. He had a stupid look of well-practiced confidence painted on his equally stupid face. He was, perhaps, Felix's least favorite of the idiots. His mediocrity never seemed to faze him. He was not hungry for greatness.

"O.K. So I see a student turning on this new stereo in his dorm room. The sound is huge. The walls shake. Books fall to the floor. The guy has a hard time walking in the quake of this sound. Won't he think he's the big man?" Lance smiled and Felix noticed that one of his eyes squinted in a particularly distasteful manner. It made him think of a pervert at the late night train station.

"Who hired you? Do you even try? You fail to have any feeling at all in your ads. Yes, this might be cute, but cute is not our goal. You want to do the ridiculous, and it is ridiculous, because the stereo will not shake the floor! Damn it. This is a waste of our time. Go get lunch and chat with other soulless imbeciles over a turkey club, because you are hollow and the ad is void. Out!" Felix tossed back a gulp of his bourbon and rubbed his temples.

"Next."

Felix's final victim presented himself. His name was Robert. He didn't always make Felix feel as though vomit was on the horizon, but there was this saccharine quality to his writing that made Felix reach for an antacid even before the man began to speak. He washed it down with a chug from his frosted vessel.

"I thought we could do something really elegant. Let's have the stereo play a beautiful classical piece, and show the music notes floating in the air. And then we'll have a ballerina dance in a circle around the stereo while it's balanced on one of those Greek pedestals. Maybe we could pan out to see an orchestra in the pit. Get this, without their instruments! Playing the song, right?"

The man got too excited. Felix needed him to calm down and think of the logistics. It was a nice idea, but who is going to pay an entire orchestra to not play?

"Also," Felix continued his train of thought out loud, "It has no true heart. It's all art and no humanity. It needs to speak to what we're missing…what we're starving for. It's just too self-indulgent. You just want to impress YOU."

Felix waved Robert out of the office. He lit a fresh smoke and sat to think. The kids hadn't done terrible work, but they couldn't capture what he wanted. Felix started to wonder if what he was hungry for was even possible to convey. Was it simply too ephemeral?

How long had he been here? Had it been decades? Had it been centuries? Had he been chasing his hunger for all eternity? Felix felt, for a moment, that he must have been. It was who he was. Maybe, he ruminated, the desire was all he was.

Felix heard some ruckus in the outer office hallway and realized he'd drifted off. The light was russet and there was a slight chill at being roused from sleep. Waking always disoriented him a bit, as though the world needed to steady itself on its axis. The burbling and tittering continued to seep under the crack in his door. His watch told him that Maggie had gone home a while ago. That explained some of the foolish sounds presently causing him no insignificant pain in his temples. They spent more time with gossip and preening than with work matters. If he wanted any peace he'd have to go out there and put a little fear of the devil in them. Felix reluctantly rose from behind his desk and, with a slight hitch in his step from being in one position so long, made his way into the harsh florescent light of the offending hallway.

"Ladies…and gentlemen, what are you doing? This isn't your social hour at the nearest cheap beer establishment. What the hell is going on?"

The cluster of employees shut their mouths. Perhaps they'd thought he'd gone. But, he was always here, whether they knew it or not. They averted their eyes like reprimanded children before a powerful father. They knew they'd been naughty. They may as well have knocked their dinner plates onto the floor with their carelessness. They were always incredibly careless.

Lance and Robert pulled on the sleeve of a uniquely ridiculous secretary in order to move her away from the desk around which they were communing. She giggled, and then immediately hung her curly head. Felix uttered something between a growl and a sigh before investigating what had so captured their attention. It was a box. An unopened box. A box that at first was unfamiliar to Felix, so out of place as it was. Then he recognized its pleasingly cubed shape and small proportions. It was the stereo he so desperately wanted to sell. It was so shiny and new. The company must have just sent one over.

"About time." Felix mumbled to himself. "I'll take this now."

He gathered up the strikingly designed unit in his arms and toted it back to his office, shutting the door behind him. He wanted some time to examine this troublesome piece of merchandise, alone. Once sequestered in his office sanctuary, he poured a drink and paced in front of his desk, ice clinking, not taking his eye from the stereo. He wanted this one to be perfect. He felt driven by some powerful urge. An urge, a need, that's what he saw when he imagined the campaign. But, he couldn't quite fill in the secret that the need concealed.

Across the office, Felix's eye was drawn to a small stack of records. They were reclining in a corner, surrounded by magazines and worn copies of Machiavelli's *The Prince*, and Hemmingway's *A Moveable Feast.* He hadn't noticed those records in what felt like a century. Felix placed his lightly sweating glass on the corner of his desk and made his way to the music stack. A couple of records he didn't even recognize. Where had he gotten them? Maybe some of the underlings had left them there. Probably that squinty Lance. He seemed like the kind of person who'd come into another man's office and leave behind unfamiliar music selections.

One recording was an old friend. Felix handled it carefully. He carried it back to his desk and placed it on the stereo, not turning it on yet. Another bourbon would go nicely with what he wanted to hear. Felix set the arm to the piece he was feeling and sat back in his chair. The sky was shifting a deeper gray as the first muted stars took up their positions, like dancers awaiting the curtain rise at the ballet. He turned the stereo on.

Haunting music, from a humid, honeysuckle-laden night filled his head. A young man, who wanted one thing only, walked down an unpaved and dusty road. Felix could hear the need. It was a sound that he recognized so well. The young man's song conjured a scene at a crossroads, draped in dirt and disorienting midnight shadows. He was willing to sell his tortured soul to fill that need. Felix turned the music up higher and higher, feeling the sound calling out into his own impending night. He closed his eyes for a moment.

His moment was rather abruptly interrupted when the foolish, curly headed secretary opened his door and teetered in on unreasonably high heels.

"Yes?" Felix was about to ask her, once again, what the hell she was up to when another employee wandered in. This intrusion was, remarkably, followed by those man-boys, Robert and Lance. They said nothing. As one final staff member emerged through his office door they gathered themselves together in a semicircle around the stereo, transfixed. Everything was silent, save the crossroads shadow music and the melting pop of ice cubes.

Felix jolted himself into an erect posture and observed these virtual strangers taking accommodation in his office. A minute earlier they had all been in their own spaces, doing their own tasks. Now, they were gathered together around the stereo, all slightly swaying or bobbing their heads to the surprising music. He had somehow gathered them into the same experience. They'd all needed to come there.

"Christ! I think I've got it!" Felix jumped up, breaking the musical spell. "I know the story we're going to tell. I know the heart and the need."

He lit a cigarette and dove into uber focus. This was big. It would be perfect. He knew what it was now.

"Lance, Robert, get your materials."

He peered around the room at the others standing in stunned awe. He pointed at the curly headed secretary, "You, I don't remember your name right now…Not important at this juncture. Start taking notes."

They burst into motion to gather their things and met back in a flash. They could feel the electricity charge the room. Felix's excitement had infected them.

"Our story is about coming together from our own spaces in the world. It's about a connection that is brought on by the simple act of turning on the stereo. This stereo. Even though you were all doing separate things, in separate places, when you heard the music you all gathered together."

Felix was completely inside his vision at this point. It was so clear. "We have a man turn on the stereo. It's in the den. The sun is setting outside his well-dressed windows. Everyone is in their own separate place within the house. Each one on their own, until they are called by the powerful, beautiful sound. They slowly wander in to the den and gather around the stereo. Together, they bond over the music. It glues the individual pieces with one another. It fills a need to belong in the world, to feel connected. They didn't even know they hungered for this moment, but they did."

Felix paused for a drag of his smoke and looked around to see if his audience understood.

Lance whispered, "That's it. You're right."

"It feeds that unconscious desire." Felix replied, knowing this was the ad he'd been chasing. He wasn't hungry in that moment. But, even with this, he knew he'd be famished again soon.

PESTILENCE

Erin Camille Jackson

I am their guardian. I am their keeper. They are the broken and disordered. They live at my will. I am the landlord to those distasteful to society. They are my charge. We are a community of the unwanted. I might be, conceivably, their devil, if they did not already have devils enough. They worship the smack, the gak, the pathetic pills (but not so much of that). They reside in the squatter house I run. Where else would they go? We are all being held captive by our personal evils. I am also held captive by these beings I house.

The squatter house has been a blight on the neighborhood's cityscape for ages. It is a wheezing, gnarled, and crooked construction that was once properly upright and fashionable. Gradually, all its neighbors have been demolished and replaced by more structurally sound units, all resembling each other, all exuding conformity and compliance. The lone force of resistance against the onslaught of gentrification has been the old lady. She loves her shithole abode more than we love illicit drugs and pilfered luxuries.

The old lady staunchly refuses to sell her beloved place at any price. Consequently, this means that our gaff, which is fortuitously attached to hers, is safe from devastation. They can neither tear us down nor remove us. We have rights, or some nonsense, to our rotten home. God bless the old bird! We show our gratitude by paying tribute, in various forms, every week. This tribute we deposit at her doorstep. As far as we go, it is a goddamn religious experience making some junkie pilgrim's progress up her front steps. This is what we do to keep our home, such as it is.

For the most part, we squatters are transient by nature, but a few of us have been here, in bitter cohabitation for eons. There is a significant hierarchy of ranks within our nest. I am, of course, as I have previously stated, the wretched ruler of these peasants. Heavy hangs the head that wears the plundered crown.

Every afternoon, when I pry open the semi-boarded up front door of our terribly narrow, multi-story abode I am miserably aware of what I am about to encounter. My nights are, more often than not, elsewhere engaged. For fuck's sake! I deserve to be elsewhere engaged for all the total shit I have to put up with from these wank bastards. And still I squeeze my abused body through the gap and, Alice like, find myself once again thrust into a hazy volatile world of utter nonsense. A wonderland of wretched creatures unable to find their way, because no way is their way. But I still go in, do I not? Because, if I bloody well do not then the fucks will all rot in their own putrid fluids and no one will pay the tribute we owe. Then where would we be? Hell…

As I enter the musty flat I am usually greeted by an odor most foul. Sadly, I have been completely unable to identify this stench, as it is both ever mutating and varying its intensity. One fine day I might catch a whiff of expired curry chips mixed with some half smoldering roll up that could only have been urinated upon by the mongrel, one eyed dog that has taken up residence under the stairwell. Another glorious day the perfume of soiled sheets dances up my nose, accompanied by mothball acridity. I know for a fact that we have no mothballs. What the fuck have the creatures been up to?

Today's smell is of mildewing news print that has found its way into a bathtub full of boiled cabbage and homemade petrol gin. Perhaps they have learned to distil gin!? Maybe there is some use for them after all. Then the hope passes. They are not capable of creating. They only destroy.

I climb up the wrecked staircase that had possibly once been painted some inane shade of mushy pea green. I deftly avoid the increasing number of missing steps and the dog shit piles to reach the first floor. There is only one room on this floor before the staircase makes a hard angle from the landing and trudges upward.

This room belongs to the "Ghost".

The Ghost claims to be named James something, but they all lie. And what does a squatter junkie's name matter to anyone anyway? We just refer to him as the Ghost because he is almost never to be seen. He comes and goes at odd intervals. A most active form of creature for a home such as ours. His room is bare and always impressively dark. He has hung black or navy sheets over the already boarded up window, just to ensure that no trace of daylight might intrude on his cave dwelling existence. There is only a splotchy military issue sleeping bag spread out across the floor. Beside it is one candle that never gives any evidence of being lit. When he, on rare occasions, is actually inhabiting this space he has a small shaving kit bag, like the ones they would give out to the wankers in First Class. It is well worn and held together with safety pins. I assume it contains his works, since there is no other conceivable place for him to store them. Today, neither shaving kit nor its ghostly master are in the room.

My blasted stomach churns as my eyes fully adjust to the deep darkness facing me. I could give two shits as to where the dodgy fellow is. That is his prerogative. However, I am here today, at this unpleasant hour, to collect each lodger's contribution to the tribute. If that spectral being has run off without leaving his share my entire evening will be fucked all to Hell trying to round up suitable filler. And then there is the matter of the flogging and stomping I will have to unleash upon the Ghost when I locate him. These vermin can simply not be trusted.

My eyes adjust. I look down at the patch of floor just inside the doorless doorway and, to my relief, there is a small pile of objects waiting for me to collect. Good. That is one contribution accounted for. In the blackness the exact nature of the tribute items is difficult to identify. I flick my tarnished brass Zippo lighter and squat like a Chinaman before them.

One slightly bruised yellow apple.

One newish looking ball of pale pink yarn.

Three roll up cigarettes.

I nod at this bounty and place the lot in my punk patch covered RAF shoulder bag. This will be well received. Time to climb up to the next floor. My knees creak audibly as I rise from my crouching position. It may rain soon.

This next floor is probably my least favorite part of our slum of a home. A new sense of revulsion, accompanied by burning bile, floods my body as I climb the stairs. I am beset with distaste for all humanity. I am trying to hold my breath as the odor of wickedness intensifies. I am deathly afraid of getting a festering splinter from the rotting wooden banister. Such an affliction is the stuff of many of my frequent nightmares. I feel certain that any splinter acquired in that dung hole would equate to a slow death not unlike that of a plague victim. I shudder.

I have arrived, and that smell is so thick in the hazy air that it is choking me. Do not vomit. Do not show the animals any weakness. They will eat you. They will cook your tired eyeballs in a spoon and shoot the blind liquid into their collapsed veins. I straighten my stance. Ready.

This floor, if I was somehow unclear, is bloody revolting. The problem, as I have come to realize, is twofold. First, the small bedroom at the top of the stairs is occupied by, not one, but *two* filthy beasts. And they have become so inclined as to romantically align themselves against the rest of the fucking world. They imagine themselves as tragic title characters in some hellish story initiated by Malcolm McLaren's creative attempts at fabulous disaster. They are thing one and thing two. Wanker and the Beast. They are often moved to attempt dialogue when on a smack ride. When they are "sober" they tend to fling all manner of inanimate objects, some clearly bio-hazardous, in the direction of their miserable conversation victims.

The second cankerous sore of our beloved living quarters is the other room on this floor. It is here that the loo resides, in all its majesty. I feel confident that from this loo escapes such rot and stink that the government has been remiss to not have weaponized it. All manner of conflicts could be resolved by merely unleashing a miniscule sample into the fray.

Now, this lavatory is technically equipped with all the trappings of any normal domestic facility. However, these are dormant objects. We have no running water. The mirror was removed from the crumbling plaster wall and destroyed years ago. The former bathtub has become a storage space for unwanted shoes and a remarkably resilient potted plant. I have no idea who scavenged the supernaturally hearty flora or even when. But, it flowers every spring. Sweet little purple and yellow flowers with velvet petals and optimistic faces. It is truly lovely.

There is a commode, but beside it sits a moldy bucket, coated with green-black slime. We keep the bucket filled with water that we steal from the neighbors' garden spigots. Poured down the commode bowl, it functions reasonably well as a waste removal device. Usually. One must be quite cautious when entering the room, as there is a sizable fucking hole just inside the door which must be straddled lest one plunge down to likely death on the floor below. This state of affairs bothers me immensely, but there is nothing to be done.

I sigh as I look past the facilities and return to my task. The bedroom before me is also lacking a door. I peer in. There they are, lying on the escaping rusty coils of their mattress. They have surrounded it with an array of candles, better suited for a cathedral than the room of two half-decayed junkies. The male of the pair, Robby, sits up when he notices me standing there. For a moment I think he does not fucking know who I am. I see the cloud pass as he manages to sort it all out in his worthless head. He flails one pasty, track marked arm at his female consort, trying to wake her. She moans. I notice her torn up vein is still spiked beneath the stained rubber tubing. It makes my bowels constrict. Well, at least she is not fucking dead, right? We have suffered that before. What an infuriatingly messy fiasco that was!

"Get up, ya' cunts. For God's sake, tell her to unspike. You people are positively disgraceful." I hate that I have to speak to them. The Ghost is seeming a better and better tenant.

"Oi, Cate…Oi! Untie and get up, why don't you? It's tribute day." Robby shakes her and, sloth-like, she complies.

They are both slumpingly sitting on their wretched island of bodily fluids and broken springs staring at my face with a brain damaged gaze. It is like someone pushed the pause button and forgot to reset the video. They are nothing but rotten wrappers, void of substance, drifting about the gutter of this world. Unthinking Id. Soon, the passing traffic will whiz by them and force their insubstantial existence into an already over-bubbling sewage drain of demise. Then I will be rid of them, right clear of their irritating presence. I sigh.

When they finally reanimate there is a rush of clumsy activity as they bumblingly search holes in their mattress for their contributions to the tribute. They are like mangy squirrels the way they stash away 'treasures' and smack. I watch as an array of filthy cotton balls emerge from the caverns of this bed, followed by a rat-eaten shoe.

Why do we have so many shoes? For God's sake, where are they getting all these shoes? And, why?

"Eh, here it is, then. Been a bit of a tight week, ya' know, right?" Robby whines, snapping me out of my footwear related contemplations. He is swaying as he presents me with their offerings.

One unopened can of tuna fish.

Three sweeties in twisted plastic wrappers

Two miniature tubes of toothpaste

"Are you sure you two do not need the toothpaste? I can smell your manky breath from down the hall. Ha!" I snatch the items, trying not to touch Robby's sooty fingers, and shove the loot into my satchel before either of them can respond.

I am out. On my way to the top floor, and my final resident. The worthless duo is free to resume whatever debauched acts of self-destruction they choose.

The top floor of our hovel is more closely related to an attic than a properly intended living quarters in that it is accessible by a pulldown ladder, through the ceiling of the floor below. It is a larger space than any of the other rooms, however, the pitch of the roof is such that it forces me, or any fellow taller than a child, to stoop slightly near the walls. I can only straighten to a respectable posture when standing in the very center of the crowded room. It is quite stuffy. And it is ridiculously difficult to maneuver among the ever growing collection of random junk that Allison, the attic room's resident, has collected. She persists in collecting despite my fervent protestations.

I agonize over visiting this part of the flat for the infuriating discovery of new acquisitions I know awaits me. Every damn time I emerge through the rotting rabbit hole into her domain Allison has dragged another filthy, broken, often smelly artifact of the outside world into that room. These disturbing additions are constantly seeking an opportunity to hobble my feet, vexing my every step.

With a rapidly expanding headache, I climb up that hazardous ladder and into the attic. I anticipate booby traps to greet me. I am not disappointed, as my first cautious steps collide me with a new trap in the form of yet another storage chest. Where does she find this rubbish?

"Fuck! Can you not at least keep a damn path clear?" I scream in her direction.

"Oh, shit. Forgot 'bout that one. Just kick it off to the side then. I'll get my tribute ready. 'Round here somewhere…" She trails off as she rustles through this amazing shit pile of a barricade.

I am tired. It is getting late and I have yet to organize my own tribute. Allison's twitchy, confused, jolting movements are amplifying the crushing pain threatening to destroy my brain. I try to distract myself by looking around this heap of junk.

I recognize her two broken hurricane lanterns, rust colored, sitting atop one of the cursed storage chests. Beside them she has constructed a palate of mismatched pillows and a remarkable number of brightly patterned quilts, scarves, and a deep blue blanket. I am reminded of images of a Sultan's bedchamber that I used to admire in an old fairy tale collection I had as a child. All she needed was a hookah pipe and a peacock feather fan. She probably had those items around somewhere.

Along one wall I notice that she has engineered a display unit out of milk crates. This is where she keeps surprisingly neatly ordered rows of dead dolls. Many of whom seem to have been involved in a death camp torture experiment. They sit with their limbless or headless bodies perched at attention in that attic prison, waiting to receive a release from this world that has so wronged them. It is a release they will never find. They are victims of the disease which has determined them to be inanimate objects. They do not live and they do not die.

"No escape for you, pretty Polly dollies. And work will not set you free." I find myself speaking out loud to their undead corpses. I am immediately, and irrationally, ashamed for my mocking words. I feel as though I might have hurt their tiny feelings.

I shake my head at my own sentimental insanity. This is where I am. I snarl in the dolls' direction. Things are out of hand. I need to hurry this along before the craziness fully takes me under.

"Christ, Allison, do let us move this along! I expect you to be ready with the loot when I show up. How can you find anything in this rat's lair?" I am now over this whole activity. The dolls, I sense, are judging me for something deeper. Something which I will never fully comprehend. It saddens me.

Out of the corner of my eye I spy another new member of her collection. I have to take a harder look to believe just exactly the abomination that stands before me. I take two steps closer and freeze. A sharp vibration surges up my spine. This crosses the line. Now, I am not thinking about doll criticism or dangerous storage chests at my feet.

"Oi! Fuck! Fuck, Allison, can you tell me what that is?" I snatch her by the malnourished, floral print covered arm and drag her violently to stand before this offending object.

"It's nothing…It's just my new treasure. It's nothing, really!"

"Allison, I want to hear you say it. Say what this is that you have knocked off the streets and dragged up into our home!" I feel as though my vision is fading out, going black on the edges. My neck vein is pulsing, ready to blow.

"It's a hat stand. I think it's lovely, not even hardly broken." She is out of my grip and wrapped around the horrible thing like a psychotic snake.

I have become rage. I have become panic. I have become violence.

"You stupid, cracked cunt. We do not have hat stands in this house. Do you know why we do not have hat stands here?" I am nearly spitting the words in her plain, freckled face. A fleck of errant saliva lands in the crop of carrot colored straw she calls hair. She either does not notice or is too cowardly to respond. I hate her even more.

"We don't have hat stands because…"

"Yes, because why?"

"Because we don't have any hats in this house. Hat stands might lead to hats." She is shaking.

"Ah, so you know this much. And, tell me, please, why do we not have any hats in this abode?" I feel my pulse slow, like a predator on the scent of soon to be devoured prey.

"We…We don't have hats because, um, because a hat placed on a bed is wretched luck. A curse on us all." She is unwinding from the wooden trunk, with its crown of curling arms.

"A hat on the bed will curse us all. And, I cannot rely upon you dismal excuses for cockroach/rat hybrids to be responsible enough to own a hat. Hence, we have no use for a hat stand, as we have no hats." I slowly and rhythmically march out the words while keeping her locked in my glare.

Fast as a whip, I grab hold of the taboo item and slam it to the ground. It cracks. I smash it to kindling under the powerful stomp of my steel toed boot. It lays there, a threat neutralized. It is a pile of harmless rubble, good for nothing but toothpicks. I am calm now.

"Allison, as punishment for this gross infraction, I am taking something extra for tribute. You learn your lesson, eh?"

She nods, solemnly. This is to be expected. She does not resist me when I choose my toll, though I can tell that it pains her some. I choose a small, cobalt blue vase with gently sloping shape and a pleasingly rounded rim. It is wider around the top and then its simple, smooth sides fall to a delicate circle of a base, making it seem at once sturdy and fragile. I cannot fathom where she stole this.

She says nothing, but hands over the rest of her tribute. I say no more, either. I climb down the ladder, carefully cradling the impossibly blue vase in my arm. Her tribute is modest otherwise.

Two miniature toy race cars.

One poorly woven pocket handkerchief.

One broken red candle.

I creep all the way to the ground floor, walk past the front door, and enter my room. It would have, in other circumstances, been the living room. It has a door that locks. It also has a sadly worn sofa of dusty rose colored velveteen, torn and hanging in numerous places. In older days it might have been the pride of the household's décor. It was probably where company sat when they dropped in for tea. I have one wooden crate, with lid, that once contained bottles of wine for transit. This is my storage and my table. There is little else cluttering up the room. I am, as I have said, not here every night.

There is nothing beautiful out in my room. I sit on my sofa/bed and stare through the darkness at the nauseating wallpaper that peels and slithers down my wall in stained strips. I think it waits until I'm out to make its progress toward the floor. I find little flecks of it littering the floor along the cracking baseboards. I do not like wallpaper. This was once patterned with enormous crimson flowers and garishly curly tendrils of vines. It makes me think unfortunate things about the people who used to live here.

I place the perfectly smooth blue vase on my crate. I touch its graceful lines and robust little body. The color is visible even in the near full darkness that has crept over my room. It is cold in my hand. There is something beautiful out in my room. I will keep this thing.

I go through my satchel and find my own tribute. I only finished collecting the items last night, and have not had a chance to look them over. It feels I am always busy. I am very tired again.

One ripe orange.

Two pairs of black socks.

One tiny ballerina from a music box.

I pick up the music box ballerina. She must have broken and been separated from her musical home. I have not fully examined her. She is very beautiful. Her position is graceful and delicate. I can imagine her spinning in miniature circles to the tune of her own private tinkling orchestra. What song would that orchestra play? I had not noticed earlier, when I found her resting alone on a rickety stone wall, but her dress was blue. It was the same perfect, impossible blue as the vase. This is surprising, since I remember thinking earlier that it was some other color. Maybe pink or yellow. It makes no difference. It is blue now, and it seems a shame to separate her from the vase. I remove her from my pile of tribute and place her upright beside the vase. I will have two beautiful things in my room.

I add a pair of torn mittens as replacement for the ballerina. All tributes are tossed together in my bag. I am nearly ready to venture out to the old lady's door and deposit these things. Finally.

Carefully, I move the ballerina and the vase onto the couch beside me and open the crate. It is not very full. I try not to collect too many things, although, now I own a cobalt blue vase and a music box ballerina. I hope I have not contracted the disease of acquiring things. That would be the curse of that infernal attic hell. But I am distracted from that train of thought. Another sickness teases me from inside the crate.

This is where I keep my works. It has been months since I indulged. Once I was much more like the worthless ones undoubtedly passed out on the second floor. I stare at the gear for a minute but, ultimately, without ceremony, I leave it all untouched. I am not like them, and I have my night to undertake. Lid closed, I place my vase and ballerina back atop and in the center. Satchel in tow, I am off.

The Ghost passes me, like a true spectre, on the front steps. He is carrying an old Smith Corona typewriter. What is he going to write about? As if he can hear my thoughts he replies.

"Someone has died. I have letters to write."

He squeezes through the door without making eye contact. I show him the same respect. His conservative use of words is refreshing after the day I have had. I continue to the old lady's doorstep with my collection of tribute.

It is incredibly dark in the street. Many of the street lights are broken, mostly busted by delinquents chucking bricks and rocks. I do not mind the shadows or the dampness that is settling in. A thin mist leaves sparkling points on my grey wool coat as I open my bag and begin to pile up the tributes, like Christmas presents under a tree.

The doorstep has a narrow roof protecting it from the mist. A large bay style front window faces the street. If she is awake and looking she can see me from that window. Sometimes I feel her watching me from within. I do not know what she thinks about this ritual sacrifice we make, but I know that most likely if I return from my evening wanderings tonight she will have taken the treasures inside. I will likely see the light of one of the candles, as I imagine she is inspecting her loot. I like to think of her being pleased with our gifts. We give so little in this life we are living. We are the takers, even at our best. We are disease and destruction, more often.

Having finished, I reverently back down the steps. Silently, I give thanks.

"Thank you, old lady, for being a stubborn creature. Thank you for staying right where you are for another day."

My nightly crawls weave their way around other boarded up buildings and down narrow alleyways. The cracking and clattering of ancient cobblestones and chalky bricks echo in the night air as my less than perfect steps knock them loose. They skitter away from me like rats, or other twitchy pests. Sometimes I even encounter a few rats who are also roaming the streets in search of something. We are alike, we night wandering vermin.

I am following one of my usual routes this evening. I desperately want my mind to be silent. It is more disturbed than usual. Somewhere, inside me, there is a rumbling disquietude that is keeping me on edge. Anxious floods of malcontent are rushing up inside me with every step. I stumble and catch myself on a concrete wall that, from its odor, must be the favorite toilet of some other night traveler. I am filled with disgust. I am so often filled with disgust.

That is what this incapacitating sensation is. It is complete disgust. This life is making me ill in body and mind. I have succumbed to the virus with which I have surrounded myself for so many years. I am in desperate need of a cure from all of this.

A nearly invisible grey cat shoots across my path. As it darts under one of the rare still-illuminated street lights I observe that it is a remarkably rotund feline, with the most peculiar powder puffball of a tail. It is in fast pursuit of one of my rodent companions. They continue their death race out of my view, without even acknowledging my intrusion into their world.

"Just another lost human creature, eh?"

I have to get away from this all. I have to disinfect my person from this life. These thoughts are pulsating at my temples like a primitive drum. The need to escape is driving my heartbeat differently than just pure anxiety. This is what I must do. There is no other way. All ways are leading me to the many forms of death a man can suffer. Death is riding toward me as I ride toward it. I must abandon the home that is collapsing around me, crushing me, crippling me. I will leave it to the contaminated humans crouching within its walls.

My pace speeds up. My feet do not betray me. I must be a sight to any that spy me tromping or, more closely, marching down the mangled road, coat flapping in the wind. My scarf takes wing and escapes into the night. I do not care. It is free.

All I care about is my deep conviction. I am resolved, in this dreariest moment, to abandon the humans under my charge. They are plagues. They sicken me and poison the air. I will set them loose into the wind. Scarf-like, I will let them sail to hell, where they belong. Where I should have left them long ago.

"I am no longer your guardian! You are no longer my pests!" I shout into the empty night.

Somehow, in my marching, I reach a main street. At first my mind is so preoccupied that I do not recognize the relatively well-lit thoroughfare, even though I come here frequently. I shake my head wildly to dislodge the momentary confusion. This violent gesture leaves me a bit dizzy, but less disoriented. This well-trafficked street is what passes for the center of our enclave. It boasts a green grocer's that has never had any produce even adjacent to fresh; a haberdashery, with dusty silk hats in the lead paned window; two remarkably similar women's clothing stores, targeting the chav clientele; a news stand, where the punks and perverts gather to plot their various mischief; and several pubs of the lowest caliber, all on the verge of losing their liquor licenses. Only a few of the pubs remain open at this hour. All the shops shut their fronts hours ago. I am aware of an enormous gnawing hunger. When did I last eat?

There is a reliably decent kebab kiosk a little ways down the wide well paved road. The food is inexpensive, even when one has to pay, and it has yet to make me ill. Also, it is run by a mustached man named Omar, who is capable of conversing in a less than bothersome manner. Omar keeps his little shop, which is not much more than a shack, open late to service the few drunks staggering out of the pubs at closing time. These days, the handful of watering holes on this street are more dangerous and degenerate than the squatter flats nearby. Omar keeps a homemade clubbing stick behind his counter and is eagerly awaiting the night he is called to use it on some fuck.

"Oi there! Where the fuck have you been the last few weeks? I was thinking you must've died off." Omar greets me with a gold adorned smile to match his gold chain adorned chest. He begins fussing about in his kiosk to scrape together something or other for me to eat.

He hands me a lukewarm kebab that I suspect may be composed of random bits of main street wild life he has murdered with his prized club. But it smells quite good. He gives me this on the house, probably because he is glad for the company. It can get lonely in the wicked night streets. Both Omar and I crave the silence in our way, but it can become both unsettling and uncompanionable if allowed to take over for too long. The mind tends to turn in on itself and does not often like what it sees. At such times, when the dark and twisted try to take hold, we find solace in the presence of another. Tonight Omar's and my twisted natures come together for a little reprieve from the dark.

I thank Omar for my food and quietly munch away as we both stare out into the empty street scene. Silent together. Something clatters in a side alley. Maybe a discarded can. A slight night breeze picks up its pace and swirls the trash collected under a rubbish bin into a cartoonish cyclone. A street light buzzes and flickers, then pops and goes dark.

Further away, a siren making its donkey call is absorbed by some other place's night air. It is silent again.

"I am finished with all of it, you know." I speak softly to Omar, as if the night might be eavesdropping on a secret confession.

"Ha. This isn't the first time I've heard you say that. It's not even the fifth or sixth, you liar." Omar lit a clove and pulled in the rich stinkingly sweet smoke. Ashes fell onto his stained shirt front.

This might be true. I have thought about ridding myself of these burdens before. But, I feel that this time there is something different in my conviction. Omar is a man of little faith. He is trapped by his own plagues of place and time. He is blighted by this kiosk and the nighttime curse of drunkards and rodents.

At this moment I hear a pitter patter of tiny furry feet across the greasy pavement. Out of the shadows emerges the fat grey cat. She waddles toward the kiosk with a clear purpose. Her progress is somewhat impeded by the burden of a hefty, pink tailed rat gripped in her snaggle-toothed, fanged jaws. She sidles up to the door of Omar's kebab stand and plops her kill right by the little side door. Her mouth now empty, she utters an insistent cry, clearly meant to summon Omar's attentions.

"Miss Kitty, you're early tonight. Happy hunting, I see." Omar opens the door and bends closer to the chimney smoke colored cat's perky little face. She meows again and, without further acknowledgement, she turns and saunters off down the street. Somewhat to my dismay I watch Omar scoop up the dead rodent with his bare hands and disappear it somewhere in the kiosk. It seems a regular thing. How often has this ceremony been performed? It occurs to me that the cat and I have both offered tribute tonight. This reminds me of my intentions. I should hasten to my purpose. Procrastination weakens resolve.

"I should go."

"You *should* go. You should go far and fast. You should not hesitate for even a moment. And you should cure yourself of this diseased life you've been living." Omar blindly packs up some mystery meat treats in a wax paper sack and hands it to me. He knows I leave this package on the broken table by the stairs in the squatter house so the miserable fucks will have at least something to eat. I always do this.

"I am going away this time. This does not have to be the way it is. I will leave them their poison palace and not care fuck all." I take the package from Omar and give him a wink and nod as I turn to wind my way back home through the night. I need to collect my things.

There is something translucent and glittering about escape. It feels like breathing, with new lungs, the clean, cool air of some garden springtime. I find my gait to be quicker and more buoyant. I have made up my mind. I am resolved. Now all that remains is to go away. I can be cured by simply closing, forever, that broken front door behind me. I will vanish, leaving behind nothing but a ghost image of someone who might have been. I will thrust myself fully into the world as a creature newly created, unencumbered by yesterday's stories and stagnant regrettable characters. I can cast off the bondage of squalor-laden missteps. I will leave it all.

***

As I enter the musty flat I am usually greeted by an odor most foul. Today, I am able to identify this odor as a collaboration between stale cider, rotting wood, and stagnant urine. It is a sharp, biting stench. It burns my nostrils. I wonder how long I can hold my breath before collapsing into a puddle and sliding down the steps, slime-like. I sadly feel that it would not be long at all. I climb the hazardous stairs in the darkness.

It is tribute day. I am here to collect the offerings of these vile humans. I am afflicted with the sickness of them and the sickness of this place. I have absorbed the germ of desolation and I have become one with it. I am here. It seems that this is a terminal condition. I am, and remain, here in Hell.

I climb the hazardous stairs in the darkness.

And I get nowhere.

DEATH

Erin Camille Jackson

He was larger than life and took up all the air in the room, reducing everyone else to dizzy Lilliputians, swooning before his luminous presence, uncertain as to how they'd arrived at this particular juncture in their otherwise muted beige lives. And then he would speak. Any clouds of lingering trepidation would evaporate and the calming certainty with which he professed his word would envelop the penitent masses, transforming doubt into ecstasy.

One miserable night he'd arrived amidst a sudden torrential downpour. The rain had soaked and then flooded the narrow valley between two limestone mountain cliffs. A stream that formerly babbled and somersaulted through the pass had gorged itself. It had become a furious, roaring, whitewater beast, crashing over boulders and felling young pine trees as it went. The raging water flow and the wicked lightning deafened the night as he began staking and hoisting his gleaming white tent against the blackened sky.

By the time the first lavender light of morning was cautiously crawling up from under the earth where it slept, and pushing away the last wisps of night, he had erected his canvas-clothed structure. The ground was squelchy with thick red clay mud, dappled by passively reflective puddles. It caked the soles of his scuffed boots and tried to suck him down into its heavy bog. He moved deliberately around the tent, checking for the third time that the structure was holding fast. He nodded in silent satisfaction at the soundness of it before reaching in his white suit coat pocket to retrieve a cigarette and tiny wooden box of matches. The crackle of flame broke the silence of the fledgling morning, flashing a golden light across his sharp features. Upon exhale, feathery tendrils of smoke lifted and danced in the air before disappearing like spirits of the dawn.

***

The tent was filled to its corners with citizens of the barely existent town nestled in the shaded crook of the valley a couple miles away. These hardworking people of ancient stock had trekked their way to the recently erected Temple of the True and Glorious Word in order to discern for themselves whether or not this peculiar, lanky stranger was worth anything at all. Many seemingly similar strangers had come to their valley before, hoping to endear themselves to these people who had carved out a sometimes miserable and desperate life from its red clay and limestone bones. The congregation that had gathered under the welcome shade of this particular tent were impressed by the electric spark this newcomer ignited in the humid air. They couldn't help but look upon his visage with curiosity and childlike adoration as he stood, elevated from them, on a makeshift wooden stage. He gleamed against the backdrop of a world that provided no source for radiance. A light turned on amidst bleak grayness. And then he began to speak.

"Ladies and gentlemen, now may I have your attentions for just a few moments. I appreciate y'all coming out here today, on your day of rest. And I appreciate the heavens for ceasing their weeping and gracing us with the glorious sunshine this morning." There was a murmur of agreement accompanied by scattered applause, for it was a splendid golden morning at that.

"Now, you don't know me. My name is Zebadiah, and I've only just arrived in your lovely town. And, know that it is lovely indeed. Why I said to myself, even as I was doing great battle with the elements of wind and rain while trying to erect this here shelter (and I truly hope you will all consider it such), I said, 'This is a blessed place in this wondrous world!' I did."

He raised his hands to the air and slowly spun around where he stood, gesturing at the trees, and valley, and sparkling puddles drying in the sunlight. He smiled his brilliant pearly whites at the gatherers with such joyful affection that they, too, looked around themselves in awe at the majesty of their familiar homestead. It was refreshed and re-alivened in their eyes. How had they not noticed it before?

"I also see before me a congregation of blessed people, people who are as fine and good as any on this earth. Yes, it's the very truth!" He gestured toward members of the crowd, shining that blinding smile upon each individual. The crowd rewarded his compliment with pleased nods and whispered agreement. There was the odd little nervous, flattered laugh from a people not often accustomed to praise from anyone, especially not such an enchanting stranger.

"Now, do not consider me a flatterer. I am a truth-teller. And I believe, in my sinner's heart, that I have been lead here by the Lord, that I might come to know each and every one of you good people. I am thusly called, I tell you." The cadence of his voice flowed through the gathered peoples like a condensed milk deluge; thick, and sweet, and cloying.

Zebadiah clapped his hands together, once, and raised them to the heavens, dark eyes closed against the magnitude of his calling. The shocking loudness of this gesture fractured the enthralled silence that had settled under the tent. Several of the women jumped, as though startled by a heat storm thunderclap preceding the mid-summer rains. He clasped his hands together before his starched shirt-front, bowing his head to observe them. He seemed fascinated by these hands of his, for he simply stood there, transfixed. After an uncomfortable few seconds he raised his head to scan his captivated audience.

"Now, ladies and gentlemen, I do say, 'sinner,' for a sinner I *am*. I will neither deny, nor hide my indiscretions. I am a lowly sinner of the first order!"

The congregation whispered conjectures, shifting uncomfortably in their thrift store sneakers and outdated flannel shirts. Heads turned, neighbor to neighbor, with looks ill at ease. Zebadiah raised his left arm high above his head and shut his coal dark eyes. A shiver shimmied through his body. His knees seemed to buckle as his shoulders rolled backward and forward. He violently shook his head and gave way to a corpse stillness that was even more unsettling than the previous gyrations.

"But hear me out. I am a sinner. However, I am also saved! I am saved by a Lord that has seen into my wicked mortal heart and counted my trespasses. And, my brothers and sisters, their number is not few!" He paused to let this settle upon the nervous crowd.

"I have been a thief. Yes, it's true. I'm not proud of it, but I cannot deny it. I once even stole a car! It was an old, beaten up Cadillac car, and it gave me no end of trouble!"

He kept his eyes closed, but a haunting, reminiscent smile crept across his lips. For just a flash.

"I have borne false witness against my fellow man. Much to my shame! I have not always dealt kindly with my brothers and sisters. Truthfully, many have cause for grievance against me.

"I have cheated. Lord, how I have cheated! I was not a man in whom a woman could place her faith. Hearts were broken along the road to where I am now."

Zebadiah opened his eyes to scan the crowd. They were totally engrossed, if a bit nervous about what familiar evils he might confess to next. This was the prime state unto which his message should fall. He continued.

"And, in the days past, I gave in to my lusting flesh. I surrendered to the earthly carnal desires of man. I tell you, ladies and gentlemen, brothers and sisters, I was a fornicator! I was a fornicator! Do not doubt it for one minute. I fornicated with women of ill repute, in houses of sin and dilapidation. I fornicated with my neighbor's wife…her name was Cecily. And then I lied about it! My good brethren, I say unto you that I have so sinned against the holy word of the Lord that I once seduced a <u>priest</u>!" There arose a sucking gasp from the shocked and absorbed townspeople. It was as though they'd collectively been struck from behind by a two-by-four chunk of lumber. They were dizzy.

"It's true. I, with great pleasure, picked up a hitchhiking priest along the highway, deep in the ocean-breezed Southern swamplands. I saw a weakness in his innocent wondering eyes and I attacked it with my wicked lust! I tell you, I seduced this most holy man of the Lord to wantonly betray his sacred vows in exchange for carnal mortal pleasures. And I fornicated with this priest, in that beaten up Cadillac car, on the side of the salty, broken, asphalt highway. And then, my brothers and sisters…I did it again. Just because I could."

Zebadiah's eyes remained closed, but the static of discomfort and confusion snapping between the members of the congregation tingled through the air and made the hair on his lean arms stand on end. He relished the kinetic anticipation of his sermon's next dynamic segment. He basked in the fizzy pinprick sensation as long as he conceivably could before releasing his audience from the glorious tension.

"Like I said, I have sinned. And I thought that there could be no help for me. That's when, from rock bottom, I prayed unto the Lord. I prayed as no man has ever prayed. I wept."

He turned his back to the congregation and hung his head. It seemed as though he might start weeping at that very moment, until he rallied himself and spun on his heels to face the gathered faithful with a radiant smile that extended upward to his glistening sharp eyes. The moment had come for the crescendo.

"Then, out of the bleak darkness of despair, came the glorious voice of the Lord. Praise him. He spoke to me of forgiveness and love. I grasped on to that precious hope with all that my wretched soul possessed, and I repented for my evil ways. I repented for the lying, for the stealing of Cadillac cars, for the fornicating with the wives of my brethren, and the repeated violation of that very willing and enthusiastic priest. I offered the Lord my soul and my body, if he would only save me from the path of the wicked and the damned."

He halted for a moment, squatted down into a crouch on the stage, and leaned toward the crowd. They, in turn, leaned in together as close to Zebadiah as they could get. He began again in a deep, hypnotic whisper.

"Then the Lord told me that he had a plan for me. For me, a sinner? Yes, it's the truth, he had a holy plan for my life. The Lord said that I was to take up my newly washed clean soul and go unto the people. He said that he was bestowing on me a great gift and a great burden. The Lord tasked your humble orator with healing the mortal bodies and saving the eternal souls of my fellow man!

By his grace I am able to mend those who are broken or ill, and to wash clean all sinners. It is a task I do not take lightly, my friends! But the gracious Lord has chosen me, and now he is working through me to do wondrous things!"

At this he stood to his full and impressive height. He raised both his arms to the heavens. And he stomped his foot with such a resounding boom upon the stage that it shook the hypnotized masses from their spell. He stomped again…and again. He began to gyrate his hips in a hula hoop circle, all the while pumping his up raised arms like pistons toward the shining white tent's peak. His head shook from side to side, dislodging a slick black section of hair, which danced back and forth across his brow.

"I say…Praise be the Lord!"

An echo rang out through the tent. It thundered against the pallid limestone cliffs of the valley and rippled the stagnant puddle waters. It rose on high, into the air, unimpeded by the earth's gravity. It returned to Zebadiah's perked ear.

"Praise be the Lord!"

The congregation had responded. It was as if they had exchanged their vow for his. And, for their faith, he would reward them with his healing powers. A covenant made in that strip mined valley, between bruised and soiled peoples and the brilliant new visitor bound them together under the mid-morning sun.

"I thank you again, y'all. I am moved, deep in my soul, by your patience for my sordid tale. I rejoice in your faith! I'm going to close this meeting, if we want to call it that, by inviting y'all to join me here, next Sunday, for a full service, where I will be offering my healing powers through the Lord. Please, all are welcome."

With that, Zebadiah stepped from the stage and wandered off toward a sunbathed tree several yards away. The men and women that had gathered under that white tent and borne witness to this man's confessions slowly broke away and headed up the narrow road to their homes. They were absolutely quiet.

Zebadiah leaned his back against the chipped bark of his shade tree and breathed in its chalky, brown, dry fragrance. Bark smelled like the daylight, without the humidity. It had dried all morning as the pale, but intense bulb of sun had made its way directly overhead. He felt smoothed away inside. His sharp edges, for the moment, had stopped hounding him. And it was good.

***

"It's been nearly two weeks and Alva's arthritis hasn't even acted up once. I swear to God, she's been prancing 'round here like a fool child." A woman in gray calico, with hair like a defiant bird's nest in autumn chatted with her nearly identical friend in the middle of the toiletries aisle of the crooked little corner store. It was, in fact, the only store in the town. It was the Five and Dime, and had once been the pride of the little town, back when the town felt up to having pride.

"Hmph…Making kinda a show of it, isn't she? That Mr. Doyle, from up the street, with the gimp leg, been tellin' people he don't even limp no more when walkin' that nasty hound of his. But, he don't parade 'round like that woman. She used to be some sort of dancer, somewhere. So she says," the first woman's companion chimed in, not wanting to seem out of the inner gossip circle. She wore enormous spectacles. They must have been her husband's once. She rubbed her eyes underneath the glasses as she chattered.

"A dancer? I bet I can guess what kind of dancin'! Ya' seen those high heels she's been wearin'? I'd fall and die if I tried to walk in them," the first woman replied, but her friend was distracted by the chiming of the bell above the store's screen door as it was opened by a rather tall, lanky man in a pristine white suit.

"Shush up, now! It's him. My Lord, he's a sight, isn't he?" The second woman in the spectacular spectacles clutched her shopping basket as she cast down her eyes to the smudged mint and cream checkered floor. She said no more as a palpable sense of shame flooded her body. Her wrinkled face flushed a terrible ruddy color under the buzzing fluorescent lights.

Zebadiah had come in to town for a few provisions. He avoided the wilting collection of dilapidated buildings as much as possible for, though the community seemed grateful and atwitter at the numerous healings he'd performed, they also radiated a cold fear when they found themselves in his presence outside the tent. It was always this way. Amazement tempered with fear. Belief with doubt. Kindness with hostility.

He nodded politely to both the women because he recognized them from several Sundays at the tent. But he hurried to collect his purchases and be on his way. Too much time in town weighed heartily on his soul. He wanted to go back to his tree, and the valley, and the tent.

"Well, I truly hope to see you ladies on Sunday. Have a pleasant day, now." He nodded one last time as he exited with his small packages in brown paper sacks tucked under his arm. The bell tinkled crisply in the humid air until the rickety door clanked shut behind him.

The word, "Fornication", ran through both the ladies' minds. They blushed that blush of shame without repentance as they hurried to get on with their shopping.

***

Farther down the valley, away from the hobbled little town, on the same side of the stream as Zebadiah's crisp white tent, was a tumbled down bitty cemetery. It had been established there long before the current town was formed. It most likely appeared around the advent of the Civil War, but before people stopped being able to afford grave markers. Virtually all of the cemetery's markers were severely weather worn. Some had collapsed into mere piles of rubble, barely holding the place of their deceased masters. Others were newer, or in better condition. They stood determinedly their ground, surrounded by grizzled grass and an iodized rusting rod iron fence.

Zebadiah's white suit reflected the cool moonlight as he wandered delicately between the graves. The grass brushed against his legs and crumpled under his slow, shifting step. He carried two brown paper sacks. One had been twisted around the silhouette of a flat glass bottle of nameless bourbon with no lid. The other he kept tucked under his arm as he picked his way around in the semi-darkness, bending at the waist now and again to examine the names and sentiments etched into the memorial stones. He'd take a pull from the bottle, casually, while pausing to contemplate something known only to his night wanderer's mind.

Zebadiah stooped his towering form down to eye level with a small, well-preserved gravestone. He leaned in, putting down his larger sack, to rub his fingers over the carved words on the marker's cold face.

"Oh, Mrs. Jane Lee May, I do regret that you have passed." He closed his eyes with his hand still pressed against the stone surface.

"I am aware that you did suffer much in this life. Beloved though you may have been, your unfaithful husband troubled you powerful much. I know those pains in your head were as much spiritual wounds as they were physical ailments."

Before standing he reached into his sack and retrieved a tiny bottle of cheap scent he'd acquired at the Five and Dime. This he placed gently at the foot of her marker.

"You only wanted to feel precious and adored. That night you took all those pills you hoped he'd find you. You wanted him to save you. But, he did not. And now you rest here in the high grass, under the odd lamplight of the moon."

Zebadiah took a long pull off of his whiskey bottle and continued his constitutional between the beddings of the dead. There was only a wisp of a breeze dancing over the grass. It was soundless.

"I know you had very little time to make your mark on this earth. You never knew the sins that torment men and women. And, yet, you were smited with the pox. You were marked for death, and fell to its clutches on a Wednesday." Zebadiah placed a flower sack doll at the little girl's grave.

He continued from grave to grave, stopping at a few to offer his words and a trinket from his sack. He drank as he walked. After a time he found himself at the far corner of the cemetery, at a grave that seemed to hunch itself in shadows and retreat from the glowing moonbeams.

"I know you, Mr. Will Blane. I know you better than I know most. You are a sinner like me. We know our own. You died without seeking forgiveness for your thieving, and lying, and, finally, for killing. Your soul was not healed, for you did not ask for it to be. You rot here in this ground and you have despair, for you have not the grace of the Lord. I pray that I shall reach all the living souls of this sad town, and leave not one in the same eternity of despair that is your lot in death." He gulped the last dregs of his warm whiskey and cast the bottle against the unrepentant man's grave stone.

Zebadiah's face rose to the sky as he lifted his arms high. The moon whitewashed his sharp features and twinkled in his black eyes. After a long, deep inhale of the clear air filled his lungs to the point of pain he began to speak out, loud and low, into the night.

"I do not despair, for I have your grace. I know that I have been chosen to preserve those that are afflicted. I'm your healer!"

As Zebadiah spoke to the sky above, it exploded with tremendous thunder. A lightning bolt cracked through the blackness farther away in the valley. Yet, no rain fell. Zebadiah continued.

"But, I am in doubt. I fear that I might not be enough. Lord, I taste failure in the air every day. How can I save all these people? Do I save them? Is this just an illusion that I have used to fool myself? Am I the fool?"

He fell to his knees by the grave of the unrepentant murderer. He tossed his burdened head into his hands…not in despair, but in horrible doubt. Thunder again disturbed his reverie. The wind rose. Lightning exploded at the gate of the cemetery, sending sparks flying like fireworks among the dead.

"Oh Lord, I'll choose to believe that this is your might, telling me your will!" Zebadiah rose from his prone position. He raised his face to the unhappy sky and rallied his belief.

"I am your tool! I'm the vehicle by which you save these poor humans! I was truly wrong to doubt your plan for me. Don't fear, Lord, I'm revived. I will continue with the work you've set before me." His face felt washed rid of self-doubt by the ponderously large drops of rain that splashed over his features. It was a downpour…A deluge that chased him back to the shelter of his tent, away from the cemetery, and readied him to perform his miraculous works in the morning.

***

The rain of the night before had cleared, once again leaving only the reflective pools in the local red clay mud. The tent dripped a few crystalline drops of leftover rain just to lubricate the spiritual proceedings. Zebadiah stood on his rickety stage and stared out at the remarkable number who had gathered under his tent. The service had been underway for a while and a few of the infirmed had been healed by the preacher's marvelous touch. The congregation seemed well pleased by Zebadiah's acts of wonder.

"Now, Ladies and Gentlemen, I believe that we may just have time for one final miracle today. I ask you, who among you has a great need? Who among you is pained? Is suffering? Be not afraid! Come forward and be healed by the grace of the Lord. I am prepared to lay hands upon the afflicted soul in such need of release from this earth's terrible tribulations. Again I say have no fear!" Zebadiah waited for the many to send forth one longing for his holy handshake.

There was a great murmur in the crowd. Slowly, a frail man in sun faded overalls emerged from the herd and made his way up the aisle to the stage. His steps were like those of a man afraid of treading too heavily over a stained glass bridge. He knelt before Zebadiah and worked his soiled felt hat in in his squared hands. His face was freshly scrubbed, like some child innocent in a Norman Rockwell illustration. Too pink and pure to be really human. It was spangled with tawny freckles from the strikingly strawberry blond bottom lashes of his blank blue eyes to his narrow, triangular chin, which he shoved proudly in the air before Zebadiah and the Lord.

"Now, friend, what is your name?" Zebadiah leaned close to hear the man.

"I'm…I'm Adam. They say I've got cancer in my lungs." He coughed a little into his hand, which was regrettably still holding the felt hat. A few specks of brilliant red blood spattered on the sad head covering. Adam's face crimsoned itself with embarrassment, and he looked as if he might flee the whole scene.

Zebadiah flashed his enormous white smile toward the man and gestured for him to rise. Weakly, and with quivering uncertainty, Adam stood before the anxious crowd. Zebadiah bid him turn and face his fellow worshipers. Adam did so, but with clear trepidation.

"My friends, this man has been struck by a terrible sickness. He is weakened and tormented! I can feel his pain. But, I also feel his faith. And his faith is stronger than this disease! His faith will save him. Now let me lay hands upon this poor soul, that I may heal him through the Lord!" Zebadiah placed his slender hands on Adam's shoulders and, with his eyes clinched closed, raised his head high. Then he spoke.

"Oh Lord, this man, Adam, is one of your true flock. He has come to this blessed place to seek your grace through me, your humble servant. I can feel the wretchedness within him! He is in such pain. Oh, he is rendered dismal and near despairing. But, he need not despair! No, he need not. For your mighty grace will work through my simple hands to cure his illness and restore, I say to *restore*, his health and his soul!"

He paused and lowered his head to face the enraptured crowd, slyly peeking out of one eye just to be certain that they were caught up in the proceedings. They were completely his. They held their breath and waited to see the moment when the miracle took place. Gripping Adam's shaking shoulders tightly, he began in a thunderous tenor…

"Be gone! Be gone, you ailment of the flesh! You that has invaded this poor man's body, you do not have sanctuary here! I command you to remove yourself and set this man free. I lay hands on him to heal his broken body, and even more to purify his precious soul that he may have peace and true righteousness in his newly unburdened life. Be healed, friend, for I have removed all that sickened you. I say you are healed!"

Zebadiah pushed his hands off of Adam's shoulders and clapped them at the sky. The thrilled crowd responded with a chorus of claps and praises as Adam shuffled from one foot to the other, finally taking a deep breath. He smiled.

"Ya' know, I *do* feel better! You did it. You healed me! Oh, bless you!" He grabbed the preacher's hand and shook it with a violence before turning to walk with a bounce in his step back to his seat at the rear of the tent. The men and women seated closest to the aisle reached out to touch his clothes or hands as he passed, calling out their praises for this miracle. A few women cried dramatically into their handkerchiefs. Their husbands stomped their tired feet and nodded toward Zebadiah.

"Neighbors, the Lord be with you!"

They responded in unison, "Also with you!"

The air sizzled with a blazing white flash of lightning. A grumble of freight train thunder shook the tent. Then rain dumped down like a waterfall, liquefying all visibility. All was white light, incoming blasts, and aggressively pounding rain. Thunder rolled again.

Zebadiah seemed to become smaller. Diminished. His shoulders folded in on his grand wing span. His face fell from its radiance. The congregation became restless. Several members began gathering their simple parcels from between their feet. The air changed. It exhaled itself from the tent, and was replaced by clammy cold. Zebadiah stared at nothingness beyond the tent, into the wetness. He looked like a blind man. There was only blankness in his gaze.

The gathering of friends and neighbors started to break up. Men took hold of their wives' hands, pulling them toward the tent's open exit. A group of four ladies tried to huddle under a single umbrella as they shuffled out to their common car. The mass of the faithful began to scatter in fear of the thunder and rain. Noise and water. As they scattered, like roaches, Zebadiah crumbled in slow motion to the floor of the stage. He hung his head as a spray of rain gusted in across the tent, causing the spray to cling to his black lashes before falling down his high cheek bones. Those of the congregation remaining awkwardly picked and duck walked their way out of the flapping tent to the relative safety of their shared rides, headed back to sturdy, but impoverished homes. These homes promised to wall out the supernatural forces as well as the threatening natural elements that loomed ominously in the sky above their holy heads.

Zebadiah found himself the lone hold-out in the sloppy, mud floored tent. He remained in a pile, slumped on the stage. His face was wet. He couldn't tell if the wetness came from rain or tears. He'd known that they would run. As soon as the lightning first struck he knew that the faithful would abandon their faith. They always did. His miracles could not embolden them against the world's storms. Zebadiah felt his heart ache. It felt as though the offending lightning had reached into his chest and burned the unreliable organ to a crisp. The rain continued as the darkness deepened.

After a long interval, Zebadiah gathered himself upright. He adjusted his now damp white suit. It hung from his body like Spanish moss in humid summer weather, giving him a haggard countenance befitting his present circumstance. He proceeded down the aisle, out of the tent, into the night. Humbled. Weary. The weight of the rain caused his tent to slack. It didn't matter at this point.

Ignoring the ornery weather's persistence, Zebadiah proceeded about his task. Clearly it was time. He started to negotiate the miserable tent off its stakes. The wetness made his chore terribly troublesome, but his will prevailed in the end. After some time gripping, and pulling, and maneuvering the ropes in the rumble-rattled raging rain he managed to drop the tent. It fell delicately into the sucking mud that slowly tried to consume its graceful, magnolia body in foot-trodden pools of red-brown sludge.

Zebadiah kicked the defeated tent. It bothered him deeply. Even the tent feared the storm. It had let the mud take it, just like the people would let their mud lives take them.

"I have tried and I have failed. There is nothing more to do here. There is only weakness." He turned from the wilted tent and away from the road to town. He began to slosh his way through the valley pass, toward nothingness, as far as one could see. The rain soaked his back, making heavier every labored footstep.

***

The storm continued. Zebadiah was gone, but the rain remained. The valley flooded and returned to its raging river state. Several young trees snapped and fell to the force of the surging flood waters. The sky held its darkness against the sun. Lightning illuminated both day and night. The thunder bowled over any and all other sounds. Many of the valley's small creatures fled to higher ground. Others perished in the terrible water.

The flood made its way from the valley, over the well-trodden road, and into the town. Its waters surged against wooden porches meant for afternoon cookout socials and covered the lone sidewalk, cracked by the roots of overly aspiring pecan trees. The waters invaded crudely dug basements and seeped into pastel-colored linoleum kitchen floors. The rain continued to fuel the liquid beast as it submerged gardens of as yet unripened plots of okra and butter beans. Salvage wood dog houses drifted in the wake. Clotheslines, poles and all, bobbed down the street on waves of muddy water, tangling themselves in fallen tree branches and rusted swing sets. Mailboxes careened carelessly into the few parked cars that defiantly held their windshields above water. But all this was silenced under the din of persistent thunder that bombarded the overstressed ears of townspeople.

Most of the residents survived the terrible storm and ensuing flood. However, a peculiar phenomenon occurred. Those citizens that had been healed by the preacher, Zebadiah, fell to the will of the wettened world. One by one they died. They died suddenly, and without reason. They didn't drown or get crushed by the debris that was carried along in the dark waters. They simply fell where they stood, lifeless.

Almost immediately the rains stopped and the flood began to recede. But it left behind the dead bodies of every single person that Zebadiah had laid his healing hands upon. Not one lived. Not Alva, not Adam, not Mr. Doyle, nor any of the others. They were just dead.

***

Under a Robin's egg blue sky, in a wild flower-dappled meadow, many miles from the narrow valley and limestone cliffs, stood Zebadiah. His head was raised and basking in the warmth of the late afternoon sun. He smiled to himself and breathed in the sweet fragrance of cool grass before setting to his task.

He gathered his wooden stakes and began to pace out the perimeter for his pristine white tent. No sooner had he placed the first stake in the soft ground did the sky darken to a deep and fearsome violet-gray. Heavy bulbous clouds drifted slowly past the gentle sun, blocking out its friendly light. The sky fell dark and distant rumbles of thunder sounded. The thunder called out its intentions again. This time it fell upon the innocent meadow. A few drops of rain fell, then more. A cauterizing sizzle of lightning briefly illuminated the now black sky as rivers of rain escaped their clouds to completely soak the ground, and tent, and Zebadiah. He took no notice, but continued to haul the tent and hoist it toward the hostile sky. Water dripped from every inch of his great, tall frame. The thunder continued to increase its volume, drowning out the music of the rain.

Late into the night Zebadiah continued to struggle with the massive tent. Its water laden weight fought against his tugging and maneuvering. The rain blinded him as he labored in the darkness. After hours of tremendous exertion Zebadiah won out. The tent stood against the combative elements that so vehemently attacked its master. He rested to look at this achievement, pleased and exhausted. As he did, the rain relented and the clouds gently drifted off, leaving a clear night sky and returning the subtle aroma of grass and ballerina-like wildflowers to the warm air.

Zebadiah listlessly lit a cigarette and patted one side of the tent, relishing the silence of the post-storm night. Then, into the sky he whispered…

"And it was good."

***

The tent was as full as it had ever been. People stood with shoulders pressed to shoulders. Those in the back were on tiptoe trying to get a better view of the preacher and witness his amazing works. They had no trouble hearing his words, as Zebadiah's tremendous voice carried over them all and out into the meadow. The congregation had been intently listening, and watching, and praising like this for many hours. Several of the local men and women in attendance had been healed, that very day, by Zebadiah's touch. The summer's heat was baking and he was about to conclude the service.

"Now, my brothers and sisters, this day we have seen wondrous works done through me, by the Lord's grace. Many who were despairing are now healed. They are rejoicing! I tell you, they are ecstatic in the presence of his holy power! Praise be the Lord! We praise him and rejoice with those that he has enabled me to heal! I say, amen!" Feet stomped and praises reverberated through the humid tent.

"I am telling you to turn away from the wickedness of despair. Have faith! Do not doubt what you have seen today. Have faith in my words and my deeds! I have saved you from wretchedness. Believe in me!" Zebadiah smiled his great glowing smile at the crowd.

"Thank y'all for your time. I send you out to your homes and lives. Praise be the Lord!"

He raised his hands as the people repeated his call for praise. The tent flaps rippled a little and a few drops of rain began to fall. The people hurried to gather their things as the rain increased its pace and volume. Thunder clapped in the distance, causing some nervous cries. Lightning was the final straw. All the congregation rushed out to their cars, abandoning Zebadiah and the tent.

He watched their numbers disappear down the now mud coated road toward their quaint town. They rushed through the wildness of wind and rain, aiming at the safety of little houses warmed by little electric heaters. In, out of the fear. The meadow had already begun to flood. Water swelled over the grassy pasture, drowning the wild flowers. Delicate petals floated along the quickening waters and tumbled into miniature whirlpools of debris. The water's wrath tore them apart and sucked them into the fray.

Zebadiah crouched down in the muddy ground, amid the trampled grass of his tent. He reached his hand into the cool mud and felt it slide between his fingers. The storm was in full form now. Blackness took over. He sighed and waited in the muck for a few moments before speaking.

"Time to move on."

He rose and slowly waded his way through the storm to the first tent stake. The air was heavy with the wetness. It was not unfamiliar. He began the ritual of pulling down his tent in the lonely rain.

Baseball:

Nostalgia, Tragedy, and the Curse of the Backwards K

Aaron A. A. Smith

"How can you not be romantic about baseball?"

—Brad Pitt as Billy Beane, *Moneyball*

The game of baseball is played on that hallowed field that lies between the realms of statistical science and epic mythology. It is a game of facts and figures. And of folklore. Of history. Of poetry. It is a day-night doubleheader played all at once like the notes of a mellifluous musical chord ringing out in unison. It is a bright and balmy summer day in New York in 1927. It is a warm summer night at Petco Park in 2027. It is a continuum—generations upon generations. It is the great American pastime. The past, present, and future standing side-by-side on freshly-cut green grass. It is tradition. It is the grand old game. It is romance itself.

Baseball is perhaps the most romantic and romanticized sport of all. It romanticizes facts and figures. Decimal points. Box scores. Streaks. Cities. Boroughs. Ballparks here and gone. Childhood heroes here and gone. It romanticizes the great dynasties of the game like the New York Yankees. Teams whose stadiums bristle with World Series championship pennants waving proudly in the breeze like the banners of conquering medieval kings.

But baseball also romanticizes the tragic. The underdog. The loveable loser, suffering year after year, and every October muttering but not really believing, "Maybe next year." Baseball loves a good elegy. Baseball loves a good curse. The tales of the great curses have been told again and again over the generations, in the process becoming part of the history and folklore of the game. Part of the very fabric of the game. The curse of the Bambino. The curse of the billy goat. Now laid to rest. But with them, part of the history and folklore of the game. Part of the romance. Part of baseball. Beside the tears of joy as the Chicago Cubs win their first World Series since 1908, a twinge of bittersweet melancholy. The mournful nature of nostalgia. The absence of goats. And romantic curses.

Curses…

***

We are tied to the great curses
Intertwined with their lore
The Splendid Splinter our prodigal son
Driving a majestic liner over the right field wall at Lane Field
Donning Padres pinstripes
Steve Garvey rounding first
Arm raised in triumph
As the baseball clears the right field wall at Jack Murphy Stadium
Murphy the goat rears his head

Mr. Padre turns on an inside pitch
San Diego's favorite son
A majestic shot clears the right field wall
And caroms off the façade at Yankee Stadium
A lead in game one
A lead lost
Bases loaded, two out
Langston and Martinez.
The 2-2 pitch carves the center of the plate
Just above buckling knees
That freeze and do not turn at the strike
As the umpire's arm freezes
Somehow paralyzed to call strike three
What curse is this?
The cursed curse of the backwards K
That the box score never read
As the payoff pitch clears the right field wall of Yankee Stadium

The house the Bambino built

Baseball Life and Death

Erin Camille Jackson

Bill Buckner died today.
I didn't know him,
But I cried.

Baseball wants you to cry.
It's hard to explain,
But it gets under your skin
And becomes part of your blood.

The losses are hard.
The stories played out on the diamond
Are epic.

The little realities,
And complicated experiences

That stain our memories with
Homeruns, double plays, cans of corn,
Stolen bases, and heart breaking errors
Become part of our story, too.

We mark the progression of time
By World Series victories,
And our refrigerator calendars
Only go through October.

It's hard to explain,
But it's more than just that intoxicating crack of the bat
That lays hold of the soul.

Sometimes the ballpark lights shine so brightly
That we forget our wretched selves for a moment.
And we become the rhythm of the pitch count,

The perfect dirt under foot,

The engulfing smell of leather.

In that instant we are safe.

The Final Game

Aaron A. A. Smith

"I can tell you my love for you will still be strong
After the Boys of Summer have gone"—
Don Henley, "The Boys of Summer"

The Boys of Summer are nearly gone.
But not just yet.
They dig into the box and toe the rubber
In the long September shadows
Like hungry ghosts who do not know that their time
has passed
Hoping to end on a high note that will resonate and
carry them through to spring.

It is the last homestand of the season.
The ballpark is still as hot as a midsummer's day
But the light is wan and tired and yellow

And it glares at eye-level until it mercifully descends.

Fall light.

And the Fall Classic will soon commence.

But not for us.

Again.

The stands are half-full.

The crowd half-hearted.

The end is accompanied by pageantry and excitement.

But it is still the end.

Bittersweet and melancholy.

The last beer of the season.

The last hot dog.

The last nine frames that you never want to end.

And you mourn even as you cheer your boys

And count balls and strikes.

Because something beautiful is ending.

The season is dying.

The game will return after the dark season turns to

spring

But this season will not.

This season is dying before your very eyes

Never to return.

The Boys of Summer will return

But this particular group will not return whole.

Some you will see next year in different uniforms.

Some will wander into that wan yellow fall light

Never to be seen again.

The broadcasters rhapsodize about the season nearly

passed

And look forward to the season ahead.

I think of a wilting cherry blossom

Withering on its branch

About to fall, but not just yet

As I count the days until February

When pitchers and catchers report to camp.

Waiting for the light to change.

Sadaharu's Dream

Aaron A. A. Smith

Sadaharu was dreaming. He knew that he was dreaming. Yet the mere awareness of his state did not serve to rouse him from his sleep and force him into the waking world, as so often was the case. He felt that he could have pulled his way into consciousness had he wanted to. But he did not want to. He felt consciousness flicker at the periphery of his mind like distorted ripples of sunlight piercing the waters of a swimming pool.

Sadaharu rolled over in his sleep, turning away from the flicker of consciousness and drifting back into his dream. There was still plenty of time before the restaurant opened. The ramen, fresh vegetables, sake, and Sapporo could wait.

Sadaharu returned to the dream. Not in order to seek some deeper meaning, or some arcane insight into his psyche, or any other pseudo-scientific mumbo jumbo. He had read and rejected Freud and Jung. He didn't think their theories held much water. The former was a hopped-up pervert, trying to justify his perversions. The latter may as well have been reading tarot cards. Their science was about as insightful as phrenology. They offered faith, like an itinerant charlatan preacher that one might encounter in a Southern Gothic novel. The kind of preacher with a too-white suit and a too-white smile who brings wrack and ruin upon the holy and the unholy alike, then moves on to do the same to the next town, and the next.

No. Sadaharu believed that dreams were too random and mysterious to be understood. Even science had failed to offer a definitive explanation. So dreams remain an enigma to mankind. A flashing jumble of images and emotions. Things remembered. Things forgotten. Things that never were. And the strange wonderland logic that only exists in dreams and fairytales.

Sadaharu embraced that wonderland logic. He would have to if he were to traverse the landscapes of tonight's dream.

***

Sadaharu sat in an imperial red wingback chair, which gave him the vague sense that he was about to be the surprise guest host of *Masterpiece Theatre.* Though he couldn't recall Alistair Cooke ever sitting in a chair of this particular shade. *What the Hell, this is my dream. I make all the upholstery-related decisions.* Sadaharu leaned back, feeling the comfortable red cushions against his back. He sighed, pleased. *Sorry Alistair.*

He looked up to take in his surroundings and froze with a sharp jolt that nearly jarred him awake. Directly across the room from him, in their own matching imperial red wingback *Masterpiece Theatre* chairs, sat a wolf and a bear. They sat upright like men. The wolf was draped in a bear skin, while the bear was cloaked in a wolf skin. *A wolf in bear's clothing and a bear in wolf's clothing,* Sadaharu mused. *Fairytales and dreams.* The bear skin was far too big for the wolf and the wolf skin was far too small for the bear. They looked to Sadaharu like two Old Norse berserkers badly in need of a tailor.

Neither the wolf, nor the bear, nor Sadaharu spoke. It was a Mexican standoff of silence.

Sadaharu cast a quick glance across the room. He knew it at once. It was his grandfather's old cabin in the mountains of Hokkaido. At least it was the image of his grandfather's cabin that lived in Sadaharu's memory. The rustic yet elegant wooden walls and floor. The black cast iron pipe stove. The tall bookshelf against the back wall, crammed with volumes of history (especially classical history and World War II), hardboiled detective stories, and an assortment of Tarzan novels. An old pachinko machine in the far corner. Embers of coal burned in the pipe stove. It was winter.

How long has it been?...

A slushy, rattling, clanging sound startled Sadaharu from his reverie. He snapped his focus back to his bizarre fairytale companions. The wolf was hunched over the arm of his chair, one paw submerged in a golden ice bucket that sat on a minibar between the wolf and the bear. The wolf fished out a single rock of ice and dropped it casually into his glass. The glass was as clear and translucent as the ice, with a round bottom and a silver ring below the rim.

The wolf tilted the ice bucket toward the bear. "Care for a bit of ice, old chap?" he asked. The wolf spoke English in a fastidious, Basil Rathbone accent. Sadaharu's grasp of the English language was intermediate at best, but within the confines of his own personal dreamworld, he understood the wolf perfectly.

"Het, comrade," answered the bear in Sadaharu's dream version of Russian. "I drink my vodka straight." The bear pounded one paw against his chest and inhaled deeply. The bear sounded suspiciously similar to Dolph Lundgren in Rocky IV. Of course Dolph Lundgren was not Russian at all. He was a Swede. Playing a Russian. In a film written by Sylvester Stallone, an American. Sadaharu pondered his interpretation of the Russian language, and decided it was a bit dubious.

The wolf grabbed a bottle of Smirnoff from the bar beside his chair and unscrewed the cap. Peter and the Wolf blared from the open bottle. The wolf leaned over and poured a glass for the bear, then poured himself a glass.

"Спасибо," said the bear.

The wolf screwed the cap back onto the bottle of Smirnoff. Peter and the Wolf went abruptly silent.

"You're quite welcome, old chap," answered the wolf. He turned to Sadaharu. "Do please join us for a drink, my good man." He tilted his head and gestured toward a bottle of whiskey on a side table next to Sadaharu's chair. Sadaharu let his eyes follow the wolf's gesture. An unopened bottle of Yamazaki 12 and a clear glass sat on the table. *Yamazaki. Nice.*

But it was the object next to the bottle of whiskey that captured and held Sadaharu's gaze. It was a little glass globe and music box with a perfect tiny ballerina inside. Sadaharu stared, transfixed by the solitary and beautiful ballerina figure in her pale pink costume. Yet there was something more to the tiny ballerina. There was a deeper beauty that he couldn't quite define. *Maybe if I wind up the box…*

"Come, come, my good man," the wolf's voice snapped Sadaharu out of his reverie. "Do let's have a drink. Plenty of time to ponder fairytales and dreams and beautiful ballerinas and tragic lobsters afterwards. Your alarm goes off in ten minutes. But in here, ten minutes can seem like a lifetime. And you still have a journey ahead of you."

"A journey? Lobsters?" Sadaharu asked, vaguely perplexed.

"Yes, yes, a fairytale journey within a dream. Haven't you been paying attention? And, yes, there will be ballerinas and lobsters."

"I don't…" Sadaharu trailed off.

"Yes! Yes!" The wolf sounded very excited now. His words sped up to a fevered pitch. "It seems that you've slipped into the wormhole, my dear boy."

"Wormhole? What wormhole?" Now Sadaharu was really confused.

"Yes, quite," the wolf exclaimed frenetically. "You see, there's a wormhole that transcends time and space, dream and fairytale, and the reality of the waking world. And sometimes, *sometimes,* someone just happens to stumble in. It's a very rare occurrence, mind you, but here we are."

"So you're saying I've stumbled into some sort of inter-dimensional wormhole? Like string theory, Stephen Hawking kind of stuff?"

"More or less," the wolf said in a precise tone and leaned back in his chair.

Sadaharu absently rubbed his temple.

"Oh come now, old chap," the wolf said reassuringly. "Buck up. Everything will be fine. Do let's have that drink. Then you can enjoy your sad, beautiful, profoundly meaningful dream before waking to a new day. Come pour a glass. It's the good stuff."

Sadaharu picked up the bottle of Yamazaki and unscrewed the cap. A Scottish bagpipe version of Kyu Sakamoto's *Sukiyaki* rose from the bottle and filled the room. "This is weird," he said.

"Да," the bear laughed. He had been silent for a while. "This is weird. I am weird. Wolf is weird. You are weird. Here's to us." The bear raised his glass of vodka.

Sadaharu poured himself a glass of whiskey and screwed the cap back onto the bottle. Bagpipe *Sukiyaki* fell silent.

"Chin-chin!" the wolf toasted.

"За ваше здоровье!" said the bear.

"Kampie!" Sadaharu joined in. *This is kind of fun.*

They drank.

The whiskey was good. Very good. Even in his dream, Sadaharu could taste it. The rich, round oakiness. The smoky, peaty burn lingering in his senses.

"As I said, my dear fellow," the wolf chimed, "the good stuff."

Sadaharu set down his glass on the table. Again, the tiny ballerina in the glass globe captured his gaze. He felt drawn, almost beyond his own will, to turn the key of the music box. And when he did, his ears were once again greeted by Kyu Sakamoto's *Sukiyaki.* Only this time, the tune rang out in the distinctive, melancholy chime that belongs uniquely to music boxes.

After a few moments, the song began to change. The tiny ballerina's costumes began to change. Her world spun faster and faster. Time turned like the key of the music box.

Sadaharu watched helplessly as an entire lifetime of songs, costumes, and performances passed before his eyes. The pale pink ballerina tutu gave way to flowing costumes of black and red and burgundy and teal and blue. Kyu Sakamoto drifted into Tchaikovsky. Tchaikovsky drifted into Chopin. Chopin became Vivaldi's Winter. And Vivaldi's Winter became Yiruma's *River Flows in You.*

River flows in You. Life flows and passes like a river. Narrow in childhood. Broad in the prime of life. Narrow again at the end. There are two streams of the river. One is life. The other is death.

Sadaharu felt a deep pang in his heart as he watched the sad yet beautiful dance of the tiny ballerina. Even as he watched, Sadaharu mourned the ballerina and her dance. He mourned the ephemeral nature of true beauty. Like the brief bloom of a cherry blossom.

Yet the fleeting nature of beauty makes it all the more precious. True beauty may be ephemeral, but it is also eternal. For the light it brings into the world never fades. It is eternal in its own moment.

And then the music stopped. The moment was over. The globe went dark. The tiny ballerina was gone. Somewhere in the distant recesses of his consciousness, Sadaharu felt a tear trickle down his cheek onto his pillow.

Sadaharu felt something soft and furry nudge his leg. He looked down. A round charcoal gray cat with a fluffy snub tail sat at his feet, peering up with big, frantic, green saucer eyes. The cat butted her head affectionately against Sadaharu's leg two more times, then leapt up and perched on the arm of Sadaharu's chair. "No die, hooman," she said, rocking back and forth on her front paws. "Give me whiskey."

Sadaharu obliged. He took a sip of whiskey, placed his left pinkie finger in his mouth, and extended the whiskey-coated finger in front of the cat's face.

A crazed glare shone in the cat's eyes. She pulled her ears flush to her head as she greedily lapped up the whiskey. Sadaharu and the cat repeated the ritual a couple of times, then the cat abruptly hopped down from the chair and walked aloofly away, swishing her fluffy snub tail.

"Sorry about that, old chap," said the wolf. "That's our house cat. She's very demanding. And a bit of a lush."

"Not my fault," the bear interjected.

"I never said it was your fault. The cat's just a drunkard."

"Humph!" the bear replied.

"Well then, my friend," the wolf said, raising his glass of vodka toward Sadaharu. "One for the road, then it's time you were on your way. Daylight is approaching. Ramen awaits."

"Or else we eat you," said the bear in a gruff monotone.

"Oh, don't tease the poor man," said the wolf. He turned to Sadaharu. "He's merely joking, old chum. Bears, you know. Not the most sophisticated sense of humor."

"How dare you!" growled the bear, pounding a big paw against his chest. "Bears funniest animals in the world!" The wolf skin on top of the bear's head winked at Sadaharu, as if it were sharing a private joke with him, though Sadaharu had no idea what the joke might be.

The wolf gave the bear a sidelong glance. "We'll leave that matter open for debate after our guest leaves. But for now, one final toast to our companion before he embarks on his journey. The wolf raised his glass. "Chin-chin!"

"За встречу!"

"Kampie!"

The wolf, the bear, and the man drained their glasses.

As Sadaharu set his empty glass on the table, he noticed something in the room had changed: the wall on the left side of the room had been replaced by a sliding partition door.

"Ah, yes," said the wolf. "Your rabbit hole. Now, through the looking glass with you, Alice! It's been a pleasure." The wolf bowed formally.

Sadaharu stood up, bowed to his strange animal friends, and walked to the door. He slid open the partition and stepped through to the other side.

Sadaharu found himself standing in the shade on the porch of an outdoor tea garden. Warm light filtered in from beyond. He could feel the wooden boards of the porch beneath his feet. And beneath the wooden boards, calm waters. Ahead, a wooden bridge with imperial red handrails spanned a tranquil pond garden. A tall Shinto gate stood on the shore on the other side of the bridge. Beyond the gate, a path extended into the distance. The path was framed on either side by a line of cherry trees. The trees were in full bloom, their delicate pink flowers just beyond full blossom. The first signs of death and decay had begun to mar the outer edges of the petals. Far away on the distant horizon, a mountain loomed in the sky. There it was nighttime. A blue-white moon illuminated the snow-covered peaks of the mountain. Sadaharu felt like he had wandered into an Edo Period woodblock print.

He walked forward, out of the long shadows of the porch and onto the bridge. The light in the sky dimmed to a dark gray-blue. Winter light. A few tiny snowflakes began to descend, tumbling softly down from the crisp air above. Or were they cherry blossoms?

As he climbed the gentle rise of the bridge, Sadaharu could feel the gaps between the wooden planks under his feet. He could hear the hollow, echoing thump of his boots against the boards.

Peering downward over the rail of the bridge, Sadaharu realized that the pond was frozen. Its icy surface shimmered in the soft, gray-blue dream light. With each step he took, the gleaming light seemed to shift and flow. To dance across the graceful curves of the pond.

Koi swam languorously beneath the surface of the ice, tails swishing lazily back and forth. *Koi. Carp. Oh carp of my dreams.* They drifted beside the bridge, swam close to the sloping curves of the little islands that dotted the pond. One of the koi, a blue and white calico, stopped for a moment and looked up at Sadaharu. Then it turned and swam off, disappearing under the bridge.

When Sadaharu reached the apex of the bridge, the world went dark and silent, as if someone had cut the light and sound to a stage performance. *A dream unplugged. How avant garde.* He sensed that he was in a tunnel. He felt shifting sensations engulf his consciousness. Something that felt like water. Moss. Ice. Snow. Movement. Light. He walked through a tunnel of cherry blossoms. Then between two walls of ice. Then through a bamboo forest. Until at last he stood on a snowy path. It was nighttime. A fingernail moon and the stars pierced the darkness of the night sky above. Soft white like the snow. Two rivers flowed beside Sadaharu, one on either side of the path. The river on the right flowed forward, running parallel to the path ahead, while the river on the left flowed backward, trailing off somewhere behind Sadaharu.

Life and Death.

On the far banks of the rivers, lines of cherry trees framed the path. They too were in bloom, blossoming in flowers made of pure ice. A single flower fell from a branch. It sparkled in the starlight for a brief moment, then fell into the river on Sadaharu's left where it was swept away. Sadaharu watched the ice blossom disappear in the current, then turned forward to face the path ahead. The mountain still loomed on the horizon.

"The mountain is the center of all, and it's lobsters all the way down," said a bullish voice.

Sadaharu turned his head toward the sound. A stout, proud-looking little lobster was slowly drifting down the river on Sadaharu's left.

"I beg your pardon?" Sadaharu said.

"Never you mind, young man. I was just ruminating in your dream. It is a fine dream. Now carry on."

"Churchill." Somehow Sadaharu knew this lobster. "Your name is Churchill."

"At your service, my dear fellow. How do you do?"

"How do you do?"

"Quite well, indeed, old chap."

"But you're dead."

"Indeed, indeed." The lobster thrust out his chin. "But I have done my duty. I have served a greater purpose. And I have died with honor." Sadaharu nodded. He understood.

"I must be going now," Churchill said. "And so must you. Tally ho, lad! Stiff upper lip, my boy. Stiff upper lip. Close your eyes and think of England and so on." The lobster raised one great red claw in a farewell salute. Sadaharu returned the gesture. He would miss this strange lobster.

The lobster leaned dramatically back in the water, spreading his arms and claws outward like the Christ over Rio statue, or Charlton Heston dying in the fountain at the end of *The Omega Man* as he surrendered to the river's inevitable current. Then he remembered something. Something important. He thrashed his claws and tensed his body, halting his momentum downstream.

"Sadaharu, my boy!" he shouted. "I almost forgot the most important thing! There is a message from the wormhole: when a lobster whistles on top of a mountain, the ballerinas will dance."

"I don't understand," Sadaharu said.

"You will, my boy," Churchill said. "You will."

For just a moment, Sadaharu thought he saw the gruff old lobster smile. Not that he was really sure what a lobster's smile would look like.

And with that, the lobster raised his claw in a final salute, leaned back, and once again struck his Chuck Heston over Rio pose. And noble Churchill slowly drifted downstream past Sadaharu and out of the dream.

On Sadaharu's right, four more lobsters emerged, borne steadily forward on the river's current. While Churchill had been proud and at peace, these lobsters who continued to drift forward on the river of life carried a heavy weight upon their backs. While they were relieved to be free and alive, they bitterly mourned the loss of their friend, leader, and savior. They would never forget him or his great sacrifice. They would never forget his life.

Sadaharu watched silently as the four lobsters trudged forward on the river current and faded, faster and faster, on the horizon.

Sadaharu turned around in the faint hope of catching a last glimpse of Churchill, but somehow he already knew what he would see: something from a different dream, or different dreams, as the case may be. He saw a high, charcoal-gray stone wall and the clear night sky above. Somewhere on the other side of the wall, a lion and a man stood tense but motionless, staring into each other's eyes. The man looked up at the sky to count the stars one last time. But from where he now stood, he could not get his bearings. He was standing under a different sky…

And somewhere in that sky, far beyond where the eye can see, far beyond the earth, two astronauts drifted, out of fuel and out of orbit, into the cold and lonely depths of space. One of the astronauts was celebrating his final birthday. And his final birthday gift was a drawing from his comrade…

Sadaharu turned back around and started forward again. The way ahead had grown dark, but he could still hear the rivers flowing beside him, could still make out the faint pale glow of the snowy path at his feet.

Then spotlight beams came to life, piercing through the darkness ahead and illuminating a sprawling theatre stage and a towering red velvet curtain. The curtain drew open to reveal a group of swans arranged in precise formation, set in their starting positions, each in her place. The first refrains of Tchaikovsky's Swan Lake rose into the still winter air.

From the darkness backstage, a pair of swans emerged and took center stage. One swan

was black, the other white. Odile and Odette.

The supporting swans fluttered their wings and spun upward in swift, elegant circles, gaining speed as they ascended into the air. As they did so, they transformed into ballerinas clad in white tutus. The ballerinas began to dance to the music. Meanwhile, the black swan and the white swan intertwined their long, graceful necks and their bodies and leapt up, spinning in the air faster and faster, until they became one figure: the prima ballerina, resplendent in a shining tutu of black and white and silver and gray. In deference to her presence, the supporting ballerinas leapt into the air, twirled once, and turned back into swans. The swans flew away into the darkness of the night.

And now the prima ballerina prepared to begin her dance. She lowered her body toward the ground and took her opening pose, left leg bent beneath her, right leg extended straight forward in front of her body. She lowered her head just above her outstretched leg and extended her arm above her delicately pointed toes.

Then she began her dance. She fluttered her left arm like a wing, then spun in a smooth, gliding arc, upward to her feet. And she danced like the most beautiful swan, spreading her wings and soaring across the stage, leaping and spinning with graceful precision, capturing the flowing sublimity of the music, the desperation and power of its rising crescendo.

And then, at last, the prima ballerina vaulted into the air, both hands above her head, body spinning in a tight, seemingly weightless and timeless rotation… And then she became the two swans again. Together, the black swan and the white swan rose into the depths of the night sky far above.

And the stars burned brighter.

The red velvet curtains drew closed. The spotlights went dark. Sadaharu dragged himself up onto the stage, pulled back the curtain, and walked backstage. Right back onto the snowy path. Surrounded by darkness again.

Then another spotlight flickered to life, casting a single, focused beam of glowing white light. And in that spotlight another beautiful ballerina shone like a star in a clear winter night's sky. She stood on a frozen lake. Behind her, a waterfall plunged into the final depths of Sadaharu's dream.

She wore a blue dress, adorned with clear and blue stones and pearls that sparkled in the spotlight.

The dream world was silent. The ballerina stood perfectly still, ankles crossed in front of her, left hand grasping her right wrist. Her head was tilted delicately over her left shoulder. A gentle smile on her face. Her big, expressive eyes stared somewhere far into the distance, dreamlike in their gaze.

There was something pure and beautiful and a bit vulnerable about her pose. It made Sadaharu feel oddly protective of the girl. Particularly odd, considering the fact that he had never seen her before. Or had he?

For some reason, Sadaharu was now holding a camera. He felt like a cliché of a Japanese tourist. But the camera must have been there for some reason. *Capture the moment. It cannot last.*

A soft, twinkling, hauntingly melancholy piano tune broke the silence. Sadaharu recognized it at once. It was

"River Flows in You" by Yiruma. *There are two rivers. One flowing forward, one flowing backward. Capture the moment…*

Sadaharu lifted the camera to his eye, focused the lens on the ballerina, and snapped off a shot. The ballerina skated forward across the ice and took the picture from Sadaharu's outstretched hand. She looked at the picture and laughed. "Спасибо," she said.

Then she began her dance. She spun back away from where Sadaharu stood, onto center ice. She raised her left arm, elbow up, then fluidly leaned her body down to scoop up a handful of ice. The girl frolicked in the idyllic and halcyon days of youth. But time was passing. The moment could not last. Sadaharu could see it in the girl's eyes. He could feel it in his heart. He clung to each bittersweet, ephemeral moment as the ballerina glided and spun elegantly across the ice. Every movement was an artfully crafted masterpiece of expression and emotion. Every gesture was heartfelt and true. It was almost too beautiful to bear. And in that beauty, Sadaharu felt joy and sorrow and longing. He mourned the beauty of the dance even as he watched it.

The ballerina leapt up and spun in the air, a single arm raised above her head. Again, she leapt, this time raising both arms over her head as she rotated in a tight arc.

Now the music changed. "The Winter" by Balmorhea punctured the chill air above the frozen pond. Indeed, winter had arrived.

Again the ballerina raised her elbow, tilted her body, and reached down to scoop up a handful of ice. But this time, the act had a different meaning. Time had passed. The carefree days of youth were gone. The harsh chill of winter was in the air. The girl looked mournfully at the ice in her hands as though it were the last time she would ever see it.

She danced on, soaring across the surface of the ice, gracefully articulating her head and neck, spinning in beautiful circles like the bittersweet movement of time.

Then she leapt once more into the air, a single arm raised toward the clear night sky. And as she did, translucent wings of ice spread outward from her delicate shoulder blades. She rose higher and higher into the night sky until, at last, Sadaharu could no longer see her. But in the dark depths of the heavens, a new constellation gleamed like the twinkling beads on the ballerina's dress. She had taken her true form amongst the stars. She was a firebird of pure ice, shining in the firmament above for all eternity.

The spotlight switched off, reverberating dramatically through the silence of Sadaharu's dream like the thundering echo that inevitably accompanies the shutting down of stadium lights in a baseball movie. Then darkness. Then sound. Water roaring and crashing. The waterfall. Sadaharu felt the uneasy sensation of falling. Falling into the final chapter of his dream. The blurry, careening, disjointed, nonsensical flicker of images that cloud people's minds at the point of waking.

Sadaharu felt the ground take shape beneath his feet. The lights came on again. He was standing in the aisle at a skating rink. He recognized the scene. Not because he had been there. He had only seen video footage years later. But he knew where he was: Makomanai Skating Rink in Sadaharu's hometown of Sapporo during the 1972 Winter Olympics. It was the night of the ladies' free skate. The night that Sadaharu was born.

He tried to catch a glimpse of the competition, but now he was in a canoe on the river. The current was surging forward ever faster, flowing toward the end of the stream. The end of the dream. Flowing through Sadaharu's childhood. The course was swift and narrow. A pink flamingo waded on the shoreline. *The flamingo. That was the nickname of Sadaharu Oh. My father's favorite baseball player. My namesake.*

Sadaharu drifted in his dream memory to the baseball stadium in Tokyo. He was sitting next to his father in the Sadaharu Oh section of the ballpark, eating a hot dog. He could smell the sharp, slightly sour scent of mustard. Sadaharu Oh was stepping up to the plate. The crowd roared and pounded their thundersticks together. Oh dug in. The pitcher went into his windup and…

The river rushed on. Scattered images leapt into Sadaharu's mind. No time for full scenes anymore. Just the quick staccato flicker of images. The current of the river was too fast and the dream was about to end.

The swift and fleeting torrent of childhood. Holding a baseball. Feeling the red stitches of the seams. Sadaharu's father teaching him the grips of different pitches. Two-seam fastball. Four-seam fastball. Changeup. Curve. Slider. Split-finger…

Soba. Sadaharu's father teaching him how to make soba noodles at the restaurant. Intricate and delicate and precise like gripping the seams of a baseball.

Cherry blossoms in spring. The Asahiyama Zoo. Carp. *Oh carp of my dreams.*

The river widened, transitioning from childhood to adulthood. Now Sadaharu was careening between rocks and vague, shadowy obstacles. *More stones? Islands? Turtles?*

Moments from his life came in quick flashes like lightning. Pitching in his high school championship game with a bleeding blister on his finger, but fighting through for the win. The first twinge in his elbow that spelled the end to his childhood dream. Meeting his wife Yuki at the restaurant. His father's stroke and slow decline…

And then there was Ichiro. Sadaharu's son, named after *his* favorite baseball player. Circles…

The river grew swift and narrow again. The rocks and obstacles were gone. Flashing images surged forth again. Sadaharu showing Ichiro how to grip a baseball. How to make soba. The father taking the son to baseball games—most often to see the local Nippon Ham Fighters, but sometimes venturing all the way to Tokyo to see the Giants. To the Asahiyama Zoo again. Flying penguins in a plexiglass underwater tunnel. Ichiro laughing.

This was the current of Ichiro's childhood. The river had come full circle.

In that moment of realization, the river slowed to a gentle ebb. Sadaharu floated downstream in the moonlight. Cherry trees along the riverbank extended their branches like welcoming arms, blossoms of ice arching above the river. The snow-capped mountain still loomed far away on the horizon. Perhaps a brave lobster had climbed its peak.

Sadaharu's little boat drifted through one last Shinto Gate. A guitar riff based on the D major scale jangled through the veil of Sadaharu's dream. He recognized it after about two notes: "Dreaming" by Blondie. *A bit on the nose, but appropriate, given the circumstances.* Besides, Sadaharu had always loved that song.

Sadaharu felt his consciousness pulled back into the waking world. The world of morning and soba and sake. Blondie was playing on his alarm clock radio. Sadaharu fixed his blurry eyes on the glowing red numbers on the clock face.

But for just a moment, in the void between the world of dreams and the waking world, Sadaharu thought he saw something else on his bedside table. For the most fleeting and ephemeral of moments, he thought he saw a bottle of Yamazaki 12 and a tiny, perfect ballerina inside a clear glass globe.

www.ingramcontent.com/pod-product-compliance
Lightning Source LLC
LaVergne TN
LVHW010603100826
845148LV00014B/2822